OUR CALENDAR PARADOX

When Time Remembers

AF528354

Tanka Das

BlueRose ONE
Stories Matter
New Delhi • London

BLUEROSE PUBLISHERS
India | U.K.

For permissions requests or inquiries regarding this publication, please contact:

BLUEROSE PUBLISHERS
www.BlueRoseONE.com
info@bluerosepublishers.com
+91 8882 898 898
+4407342408967

ISBN: 978-93-7310-362-4

Cover design: Aafiya Saifi
Typesetting: Manisha Rawat

First Edition: November 2025

Prologue

"Our Calendar Paradox" is a historical science fiction and time slip love novel that merges the rhythm of Indian traditions with the enigma of European archives. The story follows Maaya, a brilliant woman from Pune with violet eyes, whose lineage is bound to the mysteries of time, and Caelum, a man with silver eyes from Switzerland, whose family has long been haunted by fractured calendars and forgotten truths. Between them sparks an immense chemistry, a love so consuming that it defies distance, years, and the fragile borders of history itself.

Together, they uncover the hidden symphony of repeating years where history folds, memories echo, and love survives across centuries. From the vibrant streets of Pune and the serene hills of Mulshi to the glistening lakes of Lucerne and the snow-clad peaks of the Swiss Alps, their journey entwines landscapes as vividly as it entwines hearts.

The novel interlaces historical depth, cultural roots, and speculative imagination, reflecting how ancient philosophies, folklore, and scientific curiosity together shape human destiny in our present year, 2025. It is not merely a tale of time, it is an exploration of belonging, of passion, and of searching for meaning when the very fabric of time begins to ripple.

This work invites the reader to walk with Maaya and Caelum across mist-laden Pune mornings, the cobbled alleys of Lucerne, and the shadowed corridors of history where fate, memory, and desire converge.

Dedication

Dedicated to my Maa and Baba, who showed me that stories live in both the heart and the pen......

Contents

Chapter One:
The Girl with Violet Eyes

∞

They whispered that in **Bhukum Gaon**, just beyond **Pune**, **India's** radiant city, the fog at dawn spoke softly to those who knew how to listen. That the trees along the banks of Manas Lake remembered footsteps long after the people who walked them had been forgotten. The hills of the Western Ghats, ancient and breathing, leaned in like curious elders, listening to the murmurs of time.

It was on such a fog-drenched morning that a girl was born beneath a sky cracked open by lightning, to a house steeped in old books, unsaid grief, and sandalwood.

They named her **Maaya**.

And her eyes, a dusky **violet**, rich like bruised amethysts were the first secret she carried. A color no one in her family, nor in all of Pune, could explain. Her mother wept quietly when she first saw them. Her grandfather, stared for a long time and muttered something in Sanskrit under his breath:

"Yugānanta lakṣaṇam."
(A mark of the end of an age.)

She grew up in a stone bungalow perched just at the edge of Bhukum, where the wind always smelled of damp earth and ghosts. Childhood meant chasing monsoon dragonflies, their wings glittering like prophecies, through the fields where her bare feet turned red from the earth. The petrichor clung to her skin like memory, mingling with the scent of ink and old paper that drifted from her grandfather's crumbling study.

Pune, her city, wasn't just a city.

It was a palimpsest of centuries, where wisdom walked beside ruin, where stories lived in museum walls, pinnacle forts and in temple steps, and where even the rain had a language of its own. Her mother, **Meera**, once a renowned Kathak dancer, now moved in silence her ghungroo (ankle-bells worn by Indian classical dancers) hidden behind a locked cupboard. Her father, **Aniruddh**, once a celebrated professor, had turned into a ghost long before he vanished. His scandal was never spoken of, only circled around like a myth too dangerous to name.

Maaya had grown up between disciplined rhythm and reckless knowledge, between the scent of sandalwood and spilled ink, between her mother's vanishing light and her grandfather's sacred obsession with time. Even as a child, she knew there was something unplaceable about her. She lived as though caught between worlds almost belonging, yet never entirely of this one.

Now, at twenty-eight, the girl with the violet eyes had just won a prestigious global research fellowship. Her name would be printed in journals. Her theories would find space in rooms where people never forgot to listen. But even in this moment of arrival, Maaya felt it: the pull of something ancient, something unfinished. Something waiting to begin.

And in the corners of her violet gaze, a quiet question flickered

What if the fellowship was not the destination…

Maaya had the kind of beauty that caught you off guard not sculpted or loud, but eternal. Her skin was golden amber, like turmeric stirred with cream. Her hair, always slightly windswept, fell in unruly waves to her waist, and her eyes, those inexplicably violet eyes, were too vivid for this century. People often stared, unsure whether they were real or a trick of light. She had been the brightest student of her batch at Fergusson College, excelling in both physics and classical Indian literature, a contradiction her professors adored. She spoke with grace, argued with elegance, and made even the driest lectures feel like revelations. Seniors envied her intellect. Peers admired her composure. Professors wanted her as a research assistant.

Yet behind her luminous presence lay an invisible bruise, a hollow shaped like a father who never returned.

The House of Timekeepers

Maaya came from a line of thinkers who were both worshipped and whispered about. The real mystery of her Pune life was always her Ajoba i,e grandfather. **Dr. Vishwajit Deshmukh**, once a professor at renowned Harvard, returned to Pune in the early 1990s and taught as a visiting lecturer in leading universities. He was revered for his brilliance, known for his eccentricities, and famously elusive. His lectures on Ancient History and Indology drew such crowds that there was never an empty seat, even standing room was scarce.

Her father, **Dr. Aniruddh Deshmukh**, had inherited the same unyielding fire. A brilliant theoretical physicist at the University of Calcutta, he was a man far ahead of his time so far, in fact, that the world around him gradually stopped understanding him. His appearance though distinctly un-Indian in certain ways often drew mocking stares and whispered jests, as if he were an enigma not just in thought but in flesh. As his research delved deeper into anomalous calendar cycles and fractures in the fabric of time, the initial curiosity turned into ridicule. Fondly, yet mockingly, he was nicknamed "Pagla Dashu"- The Lunatic Professor.

"He's brilliant," they'd say, "but he sees ghosts on dates and riddles in shadows."

One fine morning he came home to Pune on summer holidays. The first few days went very happily but slowly his brilliance began to corrode the silence. Maaya remembered the warmth of her childhood, her mother's Kathak rhythms echoing through the halls, laughter ringing during Sunday mango breakfasts, her father's playful notes left under her pillow. But it all began unraveling by the time she was eleven. Her mother, Meera Deshmukh, once a renowned Kathak danseuse, had devoted her youth to rhythm and love. When Aniruddh's obsessions turned manic scrolls scattered on the dining table, midnights lost to cryptic equations and she began to crumble.

"I gave up my ghungroos for a man who now talks to time," Meera once sobbed in the kitchen.

When Maaya was thirteen, her father left for a solo research expedition to Central Europe. And he never returned. Officially, he had died during the research expedition. Unofficially, the family never found his body. No remains, no farewell.

Only a telegram from Switzerland, and a notebook soaked in blood. Maaya's mother faded after that. Her ghungroos tucked into a silk pouch that gathered dust in the attic.

The Saffron Box

After her father vanished, Maaya found comfort in her "Ajoba's" study. It smells of teak, ink, and old time.

He once told her, over "sambar" (a dish made with lentils) and filter coffee:

"When time bends, it doesn't creak. It sings."

She was seventeen when her "Ajoba", Vishwajit Deshmukh, first showed it to her. It was just the two of them that night, dining under the dim yellow bulb on their verandah. Her mother had long stopped eating with them, her silence louder than storms. The monsoon was grumbling far away beyond the Sahyadri hills, and the smell of wet neem and turmeric leaves wrapped around the evening like prayer.

One evening over a bowl of jaggery-laced payasam (Indian Rice Pudding), Vishwajit leaned closer and said,

"You have the same spark of my eyes, Maaya. But you'll see far more than I ever could."

He reached beneath the table and brought out two things wrapped in oilcloth.

The first was a chequered iron key, heavier than it looked.

"My **1954 Chevrolet Corvette Roadster,** it still purrs if you sing to it. She's yours now. Keep her wild."

Maaya's jaw dropped. The car had always been her grandfather's second love after his beloved ancient historical paradoxes.

But the second item... that was quieter, more potent.

A saffron box small enough to fit in her lap, yet slightly too large for her hands to hold with ease sat between them. It was silk-wrapped, its corners worn, the once-vibrant threads now faded by time and travel.

Her grandfather held it gently, as if it pulsed with memory.

"This," he said, voice quiet but firm, "is older than you can imagine. I found it decades ago, in **Gyantse**, Tibet, when I had gone there just as a traveler, searching for silence more than stories. One evening, on a narrow road outside the monastery, I came across a monk who had been hit by a motor vehicle no one else had stopped. I carried him to shelter, tended his wounds, and stayed for three nights until he could walk again."

He paused, eyes misting with something Maaya couldn't name.

"On the fourth morning, just before I left, the monk pressed this box into my hands. He said it was meant to be passed only to someone who shows *seva* (service) and humanity without expectation. He told me his order had lost something sacred: a journal stolen in the night, after their senior-most monk had died protecting it. But while the journal was gone, this box remained, and it too held a secret. A thread not gold, not jewel, but a thread that carries **blood-memory across time**."

He looked directly at her.

"It doesn't hold treasure, Maaya… but something more powerful. All my life I spent on searching the secret of this box but deep down I always felt a binding thread, one that ties our bloodline to time itself. And now, it belongs to you."

She reached for it, curious, but he pulled her hand back.

"Do not open it. Not yet. Not until you *feel* time stutter."
"Stutter?" Maaya curiously asked.
"You'll know. Like when the clock ticks twice in the same second."

Then, more gravely:

"Never speak of it to your mother. And keep it away from any man who claims to understand time. They'll steal your mind before they steal the thread."

He died two years later in his sleep. The Corvette remained in the barn, covered in bougainvillaea petals, slept in their garage, waiting under a dusty blue tarp. And the saffron box, wrapped thrice, lived inside the old teak desk in the attic untouched, but not unloved.

Maaya's Pune – Friends and Memories

Bhukum Gaon. A sleepy village near Mulshi, wrapped in misty mornings and winds that whispered through tamarind trees. Maaya's stone-bungalow sat like a forgotten verse, nestled among marigold creepers, with Manas Lake visible just beyond the bend. The view from her bedroom window was a poem of deep blue waters kissing jade-green hills, interrupted only by the silhouette of distant eagles and monsoon clouds.

Her bungalow had become an unofficial headquarters for her two closest companions. **Aanya Gokhale**, the daughter of a criminal lawyer and a Gujarati astrologer, brought chaos and color. She had a laugh that cracked ceilings and a belief in horoscopes stronger than science. Every Friday, she'd barge in,

"Mau (Maaya), Venus is combusted in your seventh house. No romance this week, please. Focus on carbs."

And **Ravi Chandra**, their philosopher-sketch-artist from Hyderabad, often showed up with a new poem, a new bruise from his bike rides, or a new conspiracy.

"You think time is linear?" he once asked, half-drunk on "masala shikanji" (fresh lime soda) at German Bakery. "No. It folds. Like origami. And some people like you slip through the creases." Maaya replied.

Their lives, though vastly different, had synchronized beautifully. Maaya's home was their safe place, especially her veranda with the bougainvillaea swing, where they'd sip filter coffee, share stories of past lovers, and gossip.

If Maaya's world was a constellation, then Aanya and Ravi were her two brightest stars, fixed, unwavering, and always shimmering with a bit of mischief.

Aanya with her bold eyeliner, laugh-like-thunder, and obsession with conspiracy theories, and her mirror opposite in everything except loyalty.

"Why fall in love, Maaya, when the multiverse probably has a version of you that already did and regretted it?"

"Because" Maaya would reply, lips half-curved, "maybe I'm the version that didn't and regrets that too."

Aanya was fiercely protective. She once slapped a boy in the canteen who called Maaya "too polished to be real." Then ordered two vada pavs (Indian Burger) like it was just another Monday.

Ravi, their third musketeer. He walked like poetry in motion, always with charcoal-stained fingertips and a sketchpad under one arm. The son of a military man from Hyderabad, Ravi had inherited discipline but none of the silence.

"We're the perfect dysfunctional love triangle," he'd often joke.
"You and Aanya in platonic war, me in hopeless longing for biryani (a mixed rice dish)."

He was Maaya's secret keeper. The one she called at 2:11 a.m. when the stars felt too far and her dreams too loud.

Their trio had rhythms. They'd bunk lectures to stroll through the Botanical Gardens near Pashan, steal chai (tea) from the sociology department's kettle, argue over Tagore vs. Rilke at Pagdandi Café in Baner.

On Sundays, they rode to Sinhagad Fort, singing classic Hindi songs off-key and laughing at Ravi's retellings of campus scandals most of them made up.

One monsoon evening, as they sat beneath a tin roof at Joshi Wadewale, eating "mirchi bhajji" (capsicum fitters) and watching the sky pour silver;

"You know what scares me?" Maaya said, biting into her spicy snack.

"That we'll forget this. These days. Like a forgotten password to a better time."

"Nonsense," Aanya said, passing her a tissue.

"We'll grow up. We'll mess up. But this, this is imprinted. Like Ravi's love for aloo tikki (potato fitter)."

"Hey!" Ravi said. "Love is sacred, and so is aloo tikki."

They laughed until their stomachs hurt. The air smelled of frying oil, wet mud, and friendship too deep for words.

To strangers, Maaya Deshmukh was brilliance with grace. To Pune, she was an unfolding legend. There was something timeless in the way she walked the shaded lanes of Bhukum Gaon, fingers brushing against wild lantana shrubs, sari pallu loose on crisp winter mornings, her violet eyes looking like they remembered centuries. But for all her mystique, Maaya lived the ordinary delights of a young woman in a city steeped in rhythm.

On any given day, you'd find her lounging on the steps of Fergusson College, half-lost in *Proust*, half-listening to her friend Aanya complaining about deadlines.

"You know, Maaya," Aanya would groan, adjusting her nose ring, "if your IQ were any higher, you'd float off the ground. Like levitating."

"Only if there's filter coffee at the top," Maaya would quip with a crooked grin.

Ravi, always wearing kurtas too long and quoting Rumi as if he owned the man's soul.

"You don't just read physics, Maaya. You flirt with the particles."

But for all her mystique, Maaya lived the ordinary delights of a young woman in a city steeped in rhythm.

At college, where she studied Physics and Evolution of Science, students whispered that she had a mind like a prism refracting logic, memory, and time. On most afternoons, she would be found lounging on the stone steps under the rain trees, her fingers slipping between books of Tagore, Heisenberg, and Rumi, while her friends Aanya and Ravi filled the air with easy laughter.

Besides, her favorite escapes weren't that elite though. She loved the kandha bhajji (onion fitters) by Khadakwasla Dam, especially on rainy Sundays. She and Aanya would eat them with hot chai and dip their feet in the overflowing canal, screaming when the fish tickled their toes. On lazy evenings, she would drift to Camp on her red vespa and eat sizzlers at George Restaurant, then finish with an apple milkshake from a famous juice shop, always holding the glass with both hands like it was a relic. She loved the old booksellers at ABC street, who always saved her the first copies of rare astronomical journals.

"You know, Maaya," Aanya teased one day, picking at a half-burnt samosa, "That Bengali professor is into you," Aanya whispered one afternoon.
"Who?" Maaya asked, frowning.

"Arjun Sen. Don't act dumb. He looks like he walked out of a Satyajit Ray film."

"You mean serious, intelligent, and emotionally unavailable?" Maaya smirked.

"Arjun Sir stares at you like you're a Sanskrit riddle." Aanya rolled her eyes and said it with a friendly nudge.

"Or an unsolved particle equation," Ravi added, flicking his sketchpad open. "It's almost scandalous, darling."

Maaya only smiled, tucking a loose strand behind her ear. "Exactly. Your type." Ravi sighed. "You reject boys who bleed poetry and fall for men who talk in footnotes." "He stares at everyone. He's a physicist. Patterns are his hobby." Maaya replied with a soft smile. But inside, something fluttered. Quiet and guilty.

Every Valentine's Day, without fail, her locker at Fergusson would overflow with roses, handwritten notes, chocolates, and once, even a music box with her initials carved in sandalwood.

Among the many who adored her, two names stood out.

The first was **Professor Arjun Sen,** a visiting lecturer from Kolkata whose syllables rolled like river songs. He smelled of old ink and wet leaves, quoted Tagore at sunrise, and once left a note in her book of *Kalidas*:

"Maaya, you are the pause between lightning and thunder."

It had stirred her, once. Deeply. But Arjun belonged to the autumns of poetry, not the architecture of time.

The boldest was **Roshan Sinha** a flamboyant hotelier's son from Boat Club Road, known for his vintage bikes and painfully poetic Instagram captions.

One twilight, he arrived at the college gate with a bouquet of blue orchids and a letter written in his own blood. Yes, real blood. He had pricked a vein and used a fountain pen.

Maaya was horrified and flattered in equal measure.

"That boy needs therapy," Aanya said, folding the letter with tongs.

"And less hemoglobin," Ravi chimed in.

Maaya never responded.

After receiving the letter she quickly tucked it between pages of her dictionary. Not because she loved him. But because madness deserved remembering. Later, she kept the letter folded inside her journal, a little disturbed, a little flattered thinking why would somebody hurt himself just to impress her or really it's love! And with the passing time, Aditya eventually moved on to a social media influencer in Koregaon Park, but Maaya remained his original myth.

Whispers in the Monsoon: The Andharnban Incident

Professor Arjun Sen was not the sort of man you forget.

With eyes like monsoon dusk and a voice layered in poetry, he floated into the college like a storm dressed in khadi. He wrote equations on the board as if transcribing fate, and walked with a calm that made time watch him instead.

And yes, he watched Maaya. Not like a man watches a woman but like an astronomer glimpses a forgotten comet.

Maaya's journal would often carry half-sketched portraits of his silhouette. She once scribbled on the back of a bus ticket:

"If he is a moment, then why does
my pulse echoed him hours after?"

That year, during the early monsoons, the college organized a trek to Andharnban - the Dark Forest. Nestled deep in the

Tamhini Ghats, the path wound through mist and moss, thick with tangled roots and whispers. It was the sort of forest where sunlight came in riddles, and the rain didn't fall, it breathed.

Eighteen students and three professors climbed together. Thunder roared above like an old God murmuring secrets. At one turn, slick with algae and the frothing run-off of a hidden stream, Maaya's boot slipped.

Time fractured.

One foot gone. Her balance tilted. The scream never came.

Because he caught her.

Arjun Sen's arms wrapped around her waist, anchoring her against him. Her body collided into his chest, her palms pressed into the linen of his shirt, the sound of his breath just above her brow.

And for a moment, everything fell away.

No fog. No thunder. Just his eyes so close, so piercing, as if they remembered something she hadn't yet lived.

Her lips parted. Her eyes fluttered. The forest vanished.

He leaned in.

A breath apart.

A heartbeat.

And then

All at once like lightning splitting the dark suddenly a Pair of Silver Eyes blazed across her thought.

"Maaya!"

Aanya's voice tore through the fog like a warning shot.

Startled, Maaya jolted, stumbling back from Arjun as if his nearness had scorched her, breath faltering between memory and mist, trembling in the hush that followed.

Her friends were waiting near the trailhead, drenched and worried.

"You alright?" Aanya asked, squinting at Arjun.

"Slipped on love, maybe," Ravi mumbled, handing Maaya his hoodie.

"I- I'm fine," she stammered. Her ankle twisted slightly, but she didn't care. She didn't look back. Didn't let herself.

Later, around the campfire, she sat between Aanya and Ravi, avoiding Arjun's gaze, pretending the storm hadn't passed through her.

But in the dark of the tent that night, as the wind howled outside and the embers glowed faint gold, she closed her eyes and felt it again.

His hands. The stillness.

Even the forest seemed to hold its breath, as if nature itself had turned to witness. And then those silver eyes blazed once more, cutting through the stillness like a secret remembered too late.

"What's happening to me?" Maaya breathed, her voice barely louder than the wind. It wasn't fear, it was the eerie sense that her thoughts were no longer her own. As though something or someone was gently pulling her back from the edge of remembering.

Sleep claimed her again, but not before the shadows shifted, watching.

And through it all, Arjun Sen remained a shadow present in jokes, hints, and half-meant questions.

"Okay but admit it," Aanya teased one night, applying nail paint on Maaya's toes, "if he kissed you in that jungle, you wouldn't be here giving me foot facials."

"Or you could've had a steamy romance and a research paper in the same semester," Ravi said, dramatically flopping on the bed.

"Nothing happened," Maaya said. But her silence that followed said everything else.

Then came the winter break, and with it, the beginning of the unraveling.

Her grandfather, Dr. Vishwajit Deshmukh had been her heaven. A retired professor, he smelled of ink and sandalwood, always scribbling in margins, often whispering to the walls when he believed no one was listening. They used to spend hours together cataloguing ancient Indian almanacs and European timekeeping manuscripts in the attic before everything fell apart.

He used to say,

"Time is not a line, Maaya, it's a loop
we haven't learned to read yet."

The year he passed, Maaya stopped visiting the attic altogether.

Until now.

Late one summer night, a storm circled the Sahyadri's, and the scent of wet stone filled the air. After a petty argument with her mother about her academic obsession and slowly turning into her father. Maaya frantically climbed into the attic looking for her old notebooks and stumbled across the dusty wine bottle, a vintage red from her grandfather's cabinet. She drank not out of rebellion, but melancholy. The kind that leaves a metallic taste in the mouth. While she grabbed the bottle, a box wrapped in aging silk cloth tumbled from beneath the old teak desk, one she kept hidden from her mother. As it hit the floor a swirl of dust rose and motes sparkled in the golden light, catching her eyes with their sudden shimmer.

The moment she reached to unwrap it, a memory surged back
"Do not open it. Not yet. Not until you feel time stutter."
"Stutter?"
"You'll know. Like when a clock ticks twice in the same second."

Something about that warning clung to her skin like a shiver. But now she could feel it. The pull. Her breath hitched as emotions rushed in, thick and wordless. Drawn by an invisible thread, her fingers trembled as she untied the silk. Beneath the fading folds, the box emerged fully an **infinity symbol**, elegantly engraved into its surface, catching the light like it remembered something too.

Inside: Faded letters, yellowed research notes, a few torn books on temporal anomalies.

Her hands trembled as she unfolded a page marked in red: **"1941 = 2025 (Full Match Gregorian). Repeat cycles: 6, 11, 28. But not all are perfect matches. Some... ripple."**

There were diagrams of lunar alignments, side-by-side weekly charts, and scattered handwritten questions:

What happens when time forgets to move forward?
Are dreams echoes of fractured calendars?
What if a year repeats, not by accident, but by design?

Her grandfather had compared calendar cycles across civilizations:

The **Mayan Long Count**, with its recurring baktuns.

The **Hebrew calendar**, syncing solar and lunar reckoning.

The **Ethiopian** 13-month ancient Coptic calendar.

The **Julian**, replaced by the **Gregorian** in 1582 adjusting leap years to better fit the solar year.

He had underlined the Gregorian origin: *"Luzern. Pope Gregory XIII. October 1582. A reform born of time's betrayal."*

And then the realization struck that this is 2025! Maaya's words tumbled out in a rush, her mind racing faster than her tongue. If I go by the Gregorian calendar… then this year mirrors 1941. The thought slammed into her. What? How? Her head swam, the ground seemed to tilt beneath her feet and in that dizzying instant, the first vision tore through her.

A corridor bathed in warm yellow light. She saw herself in a mirror, wearing clothes she had never owned. There was a man tall, with silver-flecked eyes watching her like he'd been waiting a lifetime.

The next morning, Maaya woke disoriented. Her head ached, but her body tingled, as though her skin had memorized the dream. Something was calling her. And in that moment, the past was no longer history. It was unfinished business.

That day, she pulled out every one of her grandfather's notes, and for the first time noticed the signature on some documents wasn't his but her father's. They had worked together, tracing the echoes of identical calendars across centuries.

A slip of paper fell from between two pages:

"The Gregorian fracture begins at its root. Luzern.
There is no other origin."

She mapped the research into a theory so simple; it shocked her:

Time is elastic, stretched across intention. Each calendar acts as a tuning fork. When two years match perfectly not just by date, but by intention and energy timelines thin. Reality can double. Repetition becomes an invitation.

Her grandfather had believed that **years like 1941 and 2025** weren't coincidences. They were *rips in the fabric.* And Maaya somehow was born under a convergence. The dreams. The hallucinations. The way her heartbeat faster every time the word "Luzern" was spoken it wasn't madness. It was a summon.

Maaya took the notes to the only man who could help Suddu Uncle, Professor Sudarshan Jha, her mentor at Fergusson and once her father's dearest friend.

He met her in the college's observatory room, still layered in chalk dust and quiet echoes the same place Maaya had defended her research paper.

"My God," he whispered, eyes scanning the equations. "Ani (Aniruddh) was close to something and your grandfather Vishwa Sir was bothered by his lunatic behaviour. And now it's chasing you too."

"I know," Maaya said, her voice barely above a breath.

"But I must go. I must know what they saw." Her eyes didn't waver, but there was a storm behind them.

"And if anyone can convince her… it's you, Suddu Uncle."

He looked at her for a long moment. Then quietly,

"Your mother will never let you go. Not after what happened to Ani."

Maaya's jaw tightened.

"I know. If she finds out, she'll tear the house down. She'll say I've lost my mind, just like she said about Baba! She'll try to lock me in with prayers and silence. But I can't let that stop me."

She reached into her satchel and held up the small saffron box, trembling slightly.

"Ajoba gave me this before he passed. He said *this* was meant for me. Not her. Not anyone else. Me!"

She stepped closer, her voice rising with quiet defiance.

"And you know what Baba was working on the calendar, the fracture in time, the theory no one understood. And then he just... vanished. No trace. No goodbye. Only questions."

Maaya took a breath. Deep agony was rolling down as silent tear drops from her magnificent violet eyes.

"If I'm their blood, if I carry their name, then I carry their unfinished work too. I see things, Uncle. Not dreams, visions. A pair of silver eyes. Watching. Waiting. And always... always that word."

She looked up, as if the word itself might be etched into the sky. "*Luzern (Lucerne).* Amid Baba's scattered papers, and even once from his own mouth, the name of this place surfaced. Something tells me he is bound to it or to the lands around it in ways yet unseen. It won't leave me alone. I feel like... like something's calling me there."

She blinked back whatever emotion threatened to crack through.

"I must go where Baba went. I must stand where he stood. If there's even the slightest chance, I can find him" her voice broke for just a second, "then that's more than enough. For me. For Aai.(Marathi meaning mother). For this family."

Professor Sudarshan nodded slowly. Very few knew that **Sudarshan** had long harbored a quiet, unspoken love for Maaya's mother Meera. Maaya knew. But she had never resented it. He had been her quiet protector all these years.

A Love Unworn, A Bond Unsaid

They had once walked the same sandstone corridors of Delhi University **Sudarshan Jha**, **Aniruddh Deshmukh** and **Meera Roy**. Three names etched like an old ghazal in the footnotes of time. Theirs was a friendship spun out of coffee-stained pages, campus seminars, and star-gazing nights on the university terrace. They were inseparable: the philosopher, the science freak, and the dancer.

Meera was a radiant storm. Trained in Kathak since she was six, she carried rhythm in her breath and poetry in her eyes. When she danced, people stopped mid-conversation. Her lehenga twirled like a monsoon cloud. Her anklets chimed like whispers from another realm. Boys composed poems for her, professors lost their chain of thought, and even silence bent to admire her grace.

Among those smitten, Sudarshan quietly loved her the most. He never told her not in those loud, dramatic ways that love sometimes demands. He loved her like autumn loves the final leaf gently, and with reverence.

Aniruddh, on the other hand, never tried to impress. He didn't need to. He was always immersed in things that didn't belong to this era: astrophysics, calendrical anomalies, forgotten philosophies, ancient time theories. He'd talk about the Julian and Gregorian calendar overlapping the way others spoke of cricket or cinema. And Meera, whose heart pulsed for rhythm, found herself drawn toward his mind like a moth to quiet fire.

"You were born in the wrong century," she once told him, watching him scribble formulae on a napkin.

"Maybe the century was born too soon," he replied, eyes twinkling behind silver-rimmed glasses.

Sudarshan, ever the observer, had long known where her affections lay. He bore it with that trademark wit that only masked the ache.

At a friend's engagement, he had once said to a circle of friends:

"Jab Madhubala muskurati hai, sab deewane ho jaate hain… Magar Madhubala khud kis se mohabbat karti hai bas wahi toh kahaani ka sabse bada dard hai."

("When Madhubala smiles, everyone falls madly in love… But whom Madhubala herself loves is the greatest sorrow of the story."*)*

("Madhubala" is a legendary Indian actress of the 1950s and 1960s, celebrated as the epitome of beauty, grace, and charm.)

The room laughed. Meera smiled. Aniruddh hadn't looked up.

Eventually, Meera and Aniruddh married in a quiet, almost cinematic ceremony on the banks of the Yamuna River, under the soft gold of an October sun. Sudarshan gifted them an antique sundial from Italy. On the back, he'd inscribed:

"To the dance of time, and the rhythm of love
that beats quietly beneath its ticking."

And after that, he never married. He said he was too busy with books. But the truth lay hidden in the creases of old photo albums and half-finished letters.

Years later, when Maaya asked him why he chose solitude, he smiled through his thinning grey beard and said,

"Some people fall in love.
Some remain in love.
I simply… stayed."

The Departure

Sudarshan was the one who finally convinced Maaya's mother, whose eyes brimmed with tears but gave in.

"I've already lost your father to this madness," Meera had whispered to Maaya that night. "Don't let it swallow you too."

"I have to go, Aai," Maaya said, holding her close. "But I promise, I will come back."

A week later, Maaya stood at Mumbai International Airport, the hush of early dawn wrapping her like a prelude. The terminal lights shimmered overhead, cold and white, while beyond the glass walls, the world lay still except for the pulse inside her chest.

She clutched a one-way ticket to Switzerland tucked into the inner flap of her woolen coat was a satchel that smelled of old teakwood, turmeric, and something unspoken like old ink and secrets.

Inside were folded pages of her grandfather's ancient notes, the faded outlines of constellations, overlapping calendar years, Gregorian transitions, and a diary that had begun to shift even as she read it. Some days the words moved. Some nights, the sketches changed.

The night before her departure, she had sat beneath the flame tree at her bungalow's courtyard with Aanya and Ravi, nursing cups of elaichi chai and thick laughter that occasionally dipped into silence.

"So, this is it?" Aanya asked, her voice small despite her usual fire. "You're just going to leave everything? Fergusson, your mother… us?"

Maaya looked up at the flame-red leaves.

"Not leave. Just… follow something. Something bigger."

Ravi adjusted his glasses, eyes narrowing. "You've been off, Maaya. Like really off. You've been sketching maps from memory, quoting years like mantras. What the hell is going on?"

She hesitated, then opened the little brass-bound notebook she always carried. Pages fluttered until one stopped showing a mirrored calendar, where 1941 and 2025 aligned perfectly.

"My father was researching this before he disappeared. My grandfather too. I think…" she inhaled, "I think I'm next in line. Like something's pulling me."

"It's not a legacy if it breaks you," Aanya whispered, her fingers lacing through Maaya's.

"Or maybe that's how I find the pieces of myself." Maaya deeply sighed.

The silence that followed was warm and bitter, like old tea leaves left too long in the sun.

Now, waiting at the departure gate, Maaya could still hear Aanya's voice calling after her. She could still feel Ravi's hug, the kind that was tight but wordless, like he didn't trust himself to speak.

The Saffron Box sat snug in her satchel, bound in silk, with her grandfather's final instruction penned across the tag:

"Open only when time bends and your heart does too."

She took a long breath.

She didn't yet know she was not the first Deshmukh to chase the time fracture.

And certainly not the last…

to fall in love through it.

∞

Chapter Two:
The Man with Silver Eyes

∞

Time has a strange way of folding itself around certain people like the wind bends to follow the scent of jasmine, or how birds trace invisible patterns in the sky to remember where home is.

So, it was with **Caelum Virek**.

He was born on a sun-drenched April morning in **Český Krumlov**, a picturesque town in the southern Bohemian region of the Czech Republic where the streets are cobbled like forgotten verses and houses curve like painted memory. His first cries echoed between the rose-stoned walls of a 16th-century hospital, where the windows opened to the sight of the Vltava River, serpentine and slow, glinting like old silver.

His father, **Elias Virek**, was a literature professor and amateur poet, a man of sparse words but soulful depth. He raised Caelum single-handedly, scribbling poems in the margins of his son's science textbooks and reading Rilke aloud during thunderstorms. Caelum remembered those nights vividly, his father's low voice, a steaming mug of anise milk, and the sound of crows roosting beyond the windows. His mother, Maggie left when Caelum was five. Not abandoned, just gone. Claiming she could not live within "a life too heavy with the past." She had always been too ephemeral for the world: spiritual, dreamlike, with a voice that sounded like prayer. She had moved to **Fribourg**, Switzerland, years later, where she now lived alone in a small, red-roofed cottage filled with antique clocks, sandalwood incense, and handwritten pages of scripture she composed under candlelight.

His lineage was stitched with shadows. **Leonhardt Virek**, Caelum's grandfather, was once a key member of a covert collective of scientists who believed that time wasn't a straight line, but a pliable substance, capable of being rewound, mirrored, and fractured if one could decipher the calendar's hidden codes. They had failed, or so the world believed. Most of them disappeared without trace in the 1940s. His grandfather, Leonhardt, had died of a cerebral attack during a heated winter. Or so they said. The circumstances were odd. The death certificate was signed in three inks. When Elias understood that Caelum is big enough, he gave Caelum an old, rusted pocket watch, frozen at 11:41, with a note: *"He didn't die of the stroke. He remembered too much."* Elias found it on the study table's drawer of Leonhardt.

Elias died two winters later, in his sleep, eyes open, lips parted like mid-thought. When they found him, a Pablo Neruda book rested lightly on his chest, as if it had settled there to listen to his last breath. The page was still open, the words frozen in time:

"I want to do with you what spring does with the cherry trees."

There was no struggle, but a sign of pain, only that unfinished look, as if he had seen something just before the end which he couldn't believe. Something too big for this world.

At seventeen, Caelum was sent to Lugano, a sun-splashed town at the foot of the Swiss Italian Alps, to live with his mother's elder cousin, a reclusive archivist with no children, only dust, silence, and an obsession with time. The man's home smelled of old paper and vinegar polish, and his rules were as rigid as the cathedral bells' order, punctuality, and stillness. Caelum had none of these things. But with no one else willing to take him in, Switzerland became less a sanctuary than a sentence. An inheritance of absence.

Caelum's Daily

Caelum Virek moved through the world like something slightly out of tune with it, a forgotten god in a wool coat and leather boots, carved from shadow and memory, born somewhere between myth and midnight. Now, at thirty-one, the boy no one waited for had become the man everyone noticed. He was not handsome in the way men aspired to be. He was handsome in the way legends refuse to fade as if the sculptors of Olympus had misplaced one of their own in the wrong century. People didn't just look at him. They stalled mid-sentence, mid-step as if their bodies instinctively recognized a rhythm older than logic.

Despite his near-mythic quiet, *He studied* Comparative Linguistics at the University of Zurich, intending to lose himself in the elegance of dead languages. *But one lecture on* Babylonian timekeeping and proto-numerical calendars unraveled something ancient in him. What began as an academic curiosity became an obsession that would last a lifetime. He moved from language to ritual, from etymology to epochal rhythm theory, and finally carved out his niche in a forgotten corner of academia. By thirty, he had published two books, given lectures in seven countries, and became a tenured Professor of Temporal Anthropology at the University of Lucerne, a man who didn't just study time, but seemed, somehow, shaped by it. He earned handsomely, consulted occasionally for cultural ministries across Europe, and dressed in an almost militant precision dark coat tailored close, cuffs crisp, his boots always clean. It wasn't vanity. It was controlled. One of the few things he could still claim authority over.

And though he lived alone in a quiet house in Spiez, taking the early train to Lucerne each morning, his mind was rarely alone. Memory, mythology, mathematics it all blurred.

Because something about time had never felt finished to him.

And deep down, he suspected he wasn't just studying it.

He was a part of it.

Every morning, like clockwork, he walked down Seestrasse in Spiez, the small Swiss town that cradled Lake Thun like a secret. He carried no briefcase, no backpack, just a golden fountain pen in his coat pocket and a leather sketchbook tucked under his arm. The café owners opened their shutters early when they saw him coming. Not because he smiled, he rarely did but because stillness followed him. And people leaned into that.

He looked like he belonged in a world more cinematic than this one broad-shouldered, muscular, gym-toned body, and walking with the quiet confidence of someone who had nothing left to prove. With his sculpted frame and shoulder-length hair, sometimes neatly tied and sometimes rebelliously loose, Caelum resembled Thor the Asgardian God, only more mysterious and far less interested in attention. His face was unforgettable, a strong jawline, high cheekbones, and skin kissed with the golden warmth of old bronze. But it was his eyes that truly stopped people. They were an almost impossible shade of silver, luminous and deep, framed by long, soft lashes that made them seem even more surreal. There was something ancient in them like they'd seen too much and forgotten how to blink at beauty. People didn't just stare at his eyes, they felt seen by them, in ways that made them nervous.

Back on the street near his apartment, a group of teenage boys once yelled after him, half in awe, half in envy, "If I looked like that, I'd make people pay just to be looked at!"

"You sure he's not secretly in a perfume ad?" Another shouted,

Caelum had only smirked, adjusted his collar, and kept walking.

To the women around him, Caelum was pure dream, a walking mystery wrapped in wool and silence. At the university Caelum didn't flirt or charm, he existed, and that was enough. While the women admired him in awe, the men around him carried a quiet discomfort. He was a cold competition not just for attention, but for presence. He didn't have to raise his voice or show off. He simply *was*, and that made him undeniably attractive, appealing, and handsome.

At Café Zeitlos, where he had his usual breakfast, two women at the next table leaned in.

"I don't even drink coffee," one whispered, eyes fixed on him. "But I'd sit here every morning just to look at that man."

"Look at those eyes," the other murmured. "Silver, like someone dared to bottle the moon."

Elsa, the barista at Café Zeitlos, greeted him with the usual playful groan.

"You! Again! Same breakfast right?"

He nodded. "Black coffee. Two boiled eggs. No toast."

"Have you ever thought of switching it up?"

"If I wanted adventure, I wouldn't be eating breakfast." He replied.

She shook her head, sliding the plate over.

"And the pen tapping starts in three... two..."

He'd already started. Tick, tick, tick.

"Seriously," she muttered. "Why do you always do that?"

Caelum looked at her, eyes steady and strange.

"My father taught me birdcalls through rhythm. I tap to remember him. And because silence can cause memories to fade"

She said nothing after that.

He had admirers, plenty of them. The way he walked, the way his coat fell just right, and those eyes it was enough to keep whispers circling through corridors like perfume.

One morning, two young female colleagues stood by the vending machine just down the hall from his cabin, whispering with the urgency of people spilling secrets too good to keep.

"I swear, if he ever just looked at me for more than three seconds, I'd forget I had a Ph.D."

"He's too calm," the other said. "Like he already knows what you'd do to him and how you'd mess it up."

"Don't care," the first replied, biting her lip. "I'd still let him rearrange my entire thesis. You know what I mean!"

They laughed breathlessly, hands half-covering their mouths.

Caelum passed them without a word, coat swaying, eyes unreadable.

But the corner of his mouth twitched just enough to let them wonder.

Then there was Markus.

Markus was the kind of colleague who never stopped trying to be friends. Short, round-faced, with the energy of a caffeinated squirrel and a wardrobe that hadn't evolved since 1997, Markus somehow considered Caelum his best friend.

Caelum, however, considered him background noise.

"Hey, Cae (Caelum)! Let's go get a beer after work. Or coffee? Or just sit and complain about taxes. You like complaining, right?"

"No," Caelum said without looking up.

"You didn't even ask when."

"Doesn't matter. I already knew I wouldn't go."

Markus deflated, then brightened again. "What about chess? Do you even play games?"

Caelum blinked. "I tap pens."

Markus groaned. "You're the most frustrating person I've ever liked."

"You say that every day." Caleum added.

"And I mean it." Markus firmly said.

Only a handful of people had ever truly broken past Caelum's armor. And only one had ever left a scar.

Eliane, a traveling historian, had unraveled him slowly over six months of long walks through alley-lit evenings, quiet museum visits, and early mornings where she pressed her cheek into his chest before either of them spoke. Their connection was soft but consuming. She laughed easily, loved ruins, and had a habit of scribbling on napkins when drunk. He once traced constellations across her bare back using only his fingertips. She once whispered, "I think your heart beats like a different century."

But it ended.

She needed stability. He lived inside riddles. She wanted a man. He kept being a mystery.

"She was summer," he told Markus once, quietly. "I'm... solstice."

"Dude, what does that even mean?" Markus blinked.

"It means I miss her. But I would miss myself more if I stayed."

And yet, for all his detachment, Caelum wasn't heartless. He remembered birthdays without trying, left bird feathers on desks when someone seemed down, and always left the last slice of cake for someone else. Every day, he scattered seeds on his balcony for the birds, sketching them in the margins of his research notes, whispering their Latin names like spells. It was a ritual born of boyhood of evenings spent with his father, a poet who raised him alone in Český Krumlov. They used to sit beneath a walnut tree, Elias with a cigarette, Caelum with binoculars, both memorizing birdsong the way others memorized hymns.

"Birds are time travelers," Elias once said. "They remember things our clocks forget."

Caelum never forgot that. That's why he tapped his pen.

Not just out of habit. But to hold rhythm. To hold his father. To hold the sound of a world that once loved him.

Caelum was not entirely alone. In Bern, he sometimes dined with Father Reinhardt, a retired Jesuit who used to teach him Latin. Over wine and pears, they'd argue about metaphysics and the soul's ability to bend causality.

"Do you believe in reincarnation?" Caelum once asked.

Father Reinhardt had chuckled. "Only when I look into your eyes."

In Fribourg, his mother Maggie remained ethereal, always barefoot, incense burning at her ankles.

"You dream too much," she told him once, running fingers through his hair. "You inherited that from your father. But your sorrow? That's your own."

Caelum visited his mother monthly, sometimes leaving silently in the middle of the night when she spoke in tongues he could not translate. At Bern's Einstein Museum, every other

Friday, Caelum found himself drawn not to the exhibits but to the restricted archives below rooms thick with dust and the scent of yellowing pages. Through a quiet arrangement with the curator, Frau Elsbeth, who once called his eyes "troublingly convincing," he spent hours combing through wartime correspondences, untranslated scripts, and half-burnt maps, chasing patterns and fragments searching for anything that hinted why the past was starting to echo now.

He had a hunch. No, an uncanny memory.

The first time he saw her, he was eleven fevered, eyes burning with influenza, limbs too heavy to move. But the vision was clear. A woman stood beneath the crumbling archway of Vyšehrad, the old fortress that watched over Prague like a forgotten god. She wore lace delicate and war-touched and in her hands, held tight against her chest, was a weathered book. His name was carved into its leather cover.

But it was her eyes that cleaved into him violet, otherworldly, too alive to be real. She stared at him like she had waited decades for him to wake up. He had jolted from sleep, drenched in sweat, whispering a name he hadn't known until then.

Years later, sitting in the quiet hush of Café Zeitlos, he had sketched her face on a napkin with a borrowed charcoal pencil. A waitress, peering over his shoulder, smiled and said, "She looks like a woman in an old war film." He nodded without correcting her. He didn't know how to explain that she had never aged because she didn't belong to time. She was a dream that felt more real than waking.

Eventually, he stopped drawing her.

Eventually, he had forgotten.

Until now.

The Memory That Didn't Belong

A week before everything changed, Caelum had an experience he could not explain.

It happened in Zermatt, where he had traveled, supposedly, to deliver a guest lecture on ancient numeral systems something he could do in his sleep and to hike alone beneath the looming eye of the Matterhorn, hoping the clean, high-altitude silence would silence the noise in his mind.

But the truth was, he hadn't planned Zermatt.

It was Dr. Lennart Kessler, his senior colleague from the Department of Ancient Epigraphy, who had been scheduled to speak there. But three days before the event, Lennart called him in a breathless panic.

"Caelum, I know it's absurdly short notice, but Alina's gone into early labor. Twins. She's due any moment. I can't leave. You're the only one I trust to step in. Please."

And so, with one reluctant sigh and a carry-on packed in under twenty minutes, Caelum boarded the train to Zermatt.

On the second evening, a storm rolled in suddenly. The lecture had ended early. The streets shimmered wet under the streetlamps as he took a wrong turn on his walk back to the guesthouse. Drawn by the scent of pine and the hush of rain, he wandered toward the edge of the Hinterdorf Forest, a quiet stretch just above Zermatt, where tourists often walked beneath alpine trees.

Caelum wasn't looking for anything, just space, just silence. But the trail had turned slick with rain, and as he stepped over a mossy ridge, his foot slipped.

He tumbled hard down the slope, branches whipping past, until his skull struck a thick, ancient root jutting from the hillside. The world blinked out.

And then something else.

In the dark cradle of unconsciousness, he saw her. A girl, standing barefoot in the fog of his mind. Violet eyes. A soft glow. A voice not spoken but felt.

"Caelum… you will find her soon."

A crack of thunder roared in the distance. His fingers twitched. Eyes fluttered open.

Rain hit his face. He was back. His chest tightened. Because he hadn't told anyone.

Not about dreams.
Not about the watch.
Not about the violet-eyed girl who spoke his name like she already knew the end of him.

That night, for the first time in years, he began sleeping with the pocket watch beneath his pillow again.

But what Caelum could not have known not yet was that at that very same moment, thousands of kilometers away in Pune, at precisely two in the morning, a girl had jolted awake.

She had seen him.

Whispering his name like it had always belonged to her lips.

And the strangest part? It had already begun quietly, invisibly, beyond the reach of formulas or fate. Something had slipped beneath logic like a crack beneath ice, threading itself between two lives destined never to meet. No priest sensed it, and not even the most precise astrologer had mapped what was unfolding: across hemispheres and hours, two souls had started to move in unnerving synchrony.

In the alpine hush of Zermatt, as thunder light shimmered through the mist-drenched trees of Hinterdorf, a man with silver eyes awoke beneath an ancient root his pulse echoing with the memory of a girl who did not belong to this world yet waited for him within it.

And in the restless dark of Pune, beneath the swollen breath of Sahyadri thunder, a girl with a wine-heavy pulse slipped into a dream stitched from someone else's century.

It was **9:30 PM in Switzerland**. It was **2:00 AM in India**. But in that one breath, it was the same moment.

For when Caelum's fingers met the ink, Maaya's breath caught mid-sleep, as if some secret wind passed through both their chests.

Something ancient had found its way back into the present. And whatever this riddle of a man and a girl, of time slipping sideways was only the beginning of a secret the centuries had tried, and failed, to bury. What force had bound them so precisely, without ever letting them know? And if the universe noticed, why did it stay silent?

∞

Chapter Three: A Constellation Misaligned

∞

The rain had just ended, leaving behind a fine shimmer on the cobblestones of Lucerne. The sky, soaked in grey-violet hues, hung low over the sharp ridges of the Alps.

Maaya stepped off the tram in front of the Lucerne Historical Archives, her boots clicking softly against the wet stone. Her heart was restless, an emotion she couldn't explain. She had come to explore early European astronomical records, but something deeper pulled at her a strange magnetic tension she had carried for weeks.

Inside the archives, the exhibition was unusually crowded: "Chronos and the Cartographers: Mapping Time Across Civilizations." The atrium held ancient manuscripts under glass, time-keeping instruments from forgotten kingdoms, and curious diagrams sketched by hands long gone.

She moved through the hushed gallery like a ghost chasing time, the hem of her shawl brushing against marble floors that had known centuries. Dust swirled in the shafts of light filtering through high stained-glass panels, dancing in the air like celestial debris.

At the far end, Maaya paused to a faded star map etched in sapphire ink, its constellations frozen mid-whisper. 1941. She didn't know why that year called to her, only that it did. Her fingers, elegant and unsure, reached toward a folded map jutting slightly from its archival sleeve just a little more, and another hand collided with hers.

A spark. Not heat, not cold but something between waking and remembering.

"Careful," came a voice, low and calm, but edged with command. "That's an original. Mishandling it could end your access permanently."

Maaya froze, her hand half-withdrawn, pulse skipping. She turned.

The man standing before her wasn't a scholar. He wasn't a tourist. He looked like someone written into the margins of history: angular jaw, rain-damp hair falling in loose waves, and eyes that didn't just observe, but remembered. A kind of melancholy sharpness clung to him, like a violin string pulled too tight.

For a second, she simply stared. He looked like the kind of man one might have dreamt of once and forgotten until now.

"I wasn't mishandling anything," she said, finding her voice and straightening her shoulders. "But maybe if you weren't floating around like a brooding apparition"

"I was reading," he replied, dry. "You interrupted."

"Looked more like loitering with a tragic backstory."

His lips twitched just barely.

Their eyes locked. Something hummed beneath the silence, not quite recognition, but something more ancient. A pull. A thread.

"Caelum," he said, reluctantly, like the name had once meant something and had only just started again.

"Maaya," she said, quieter than she intended. Her name sounded strange between them as if it had always belonged in his mouth.

His eyes scanned her again slowly, like he was assembling a puzzle he didn't know he'd been missing.

"I've seen you before," he murmured, more to himself. "Café Zeitlos. Two days ago. You were scribbling on a napkin something about solstice reversals."

She tilted her head, surprised. "You noticed?"

"I notice strange things," he said. "Especially when they sit near the window and look like they're trying to decode the universe."

"You were there too," she replied, voice softening. "You looked like someone carrying stars in his pocket. Or mourning them."

"I was calculating planetary echo intervals," he said simply.

She blinked, half-smiling despite herself. "That's the most poetic thing anyone's said to me all week."

They stood there, the silence between them pulsing. She could feel the slow gravity of something just beginning. Like the first note of a love song, not yet played.

He stepped back, eyes unreadable. "Be careful with the map."

Then, without another word, Caelum turned and walked away but Maaya didn't move. Not yet.

Her fingers still tingled where they'd touched. Her breath had changed shape. And for reasons she couldn't name, she felt as if something forgotten had just returned.

Maaya stood still for a moment, her eyes lingering on the space where he had just been. There was something oddly familiar about him not in the way of recognition, but in the way, dreams sometimes echo into waking life. Something about the way he looked at her as if she had interrupted a memory.

And then there was the color of his eyes not just grey, but silver, like lightning caught in water. The image lodged itself quietly in the back of her mind before she could shake it off.

Had she seen those eyes somewhere before? The question flickered in her thoughts, uninvited. She caught herself, smiled wryly, and let it drift, pretending not to notice the pull they held over her.

A few steps away, down the long corridor of the archive, Caelum walked briskly, but his thoughts lingered behind. That girl Maaya. The way she stood her ground. The sharpness in her voice. The stillness in her eyes. Something about her unsettled him, though he couldn't say why. And those eyes violet, not common, not subtle. Striking like dusk before a storm. A detail he didn't want to remember but knew he would.

Both paused for a breath, in different corners of the hall, lost in thoughts they wouldn't admit aloud.

And then, without planning, without knowing,
both murmured quietly under their breath

"Silly Maaya."
"Silly Caelum."

At the exact same moment. A faint smile tugged at both their lips, though neither of them knew why.

And from the shadows near the curator's alcove, a man adjusted his coat and whispered to himself, "Right on time."

Between Time and Streetlights

The days that followed their first encounter weren't quite linear, more like threads weaving themselves around invisible spools of fate, as if time, in all its quiet rebellion, was tugging them closer.

At the corner table of Café Zeitlos, where hours stretched and folded into each other like soft echoes, Maaya found herself ordering a cinnamon-spiced black coffee the same as his. Always the same. And every other day, he would already be there, eyes fixed on a leather-bound notebook, pretending not to see her. Yet, like clockwork, the moment she passed, he would glance up once. Always once. Coincidence? Maybe. Or maybe something more ancient in motion.

Once, they reached for the same book again in the university archive, a rare copy on Julian reforms. Their hands brushed in eerie déjà vu. Another day, they stood on opposite tram platforms, studying a city map under grey skies, neither acknowledging the other, but both aware. Patterns emerged like constellations.

The next time at Café Zeitlos, inevitability arrived softly. Caelum broke the silence.

"You come here often," Caelum said without looking up, his voice dry and distant.

Maaya took a slow sip of her coffee, smirking. "You're not very original with lines, are you?"

He shut the notebook with a faint thud. "What brought you here, Maaya?"

She blinked, caught off guard. There was no sarcasm, no challenge in his voice, only quiet, genuine curiosity.

"I've noticed your eyes," he continued, softer now. "They're always searching. You don't belong here. You're not from this country, are you?"

She hesitated. Something in his gaze no longer watchful, but wide open felt safe. Disarming.

"And the other day," he added, "I heard you speak another language. Indian, I think? Hindi?"

He said it awkwardly, his accent skewing the vowels, and Maaya burst into laughter, loud and unfiltered.

"You sounded like you were ordering dessert in Latin," she teased, wiping a tear. "But it was sweet. Don't mind me laughing."

"I mind a little," he said, lips curving.

She leaned back in her chair, her eyes flickering. "I'm here for research. Gregorian calendar deviations. Time travel theories. Temporal physics."
She said it lightly, but a tremor sat beneath the words. It wasn't a full truth. But it was enough for now.

He tilted his head, thoughtful. "Well, if you don't mind, I could be of help." A pause. "Though you are annoyingly talkative." He gave her a long-suffering glance. "But your area of research aligns with mine. Who knows? Maybe I'll find some answers of my own."

Then, narrowing his eyes, he added with mock suspicion, "Or maybe you're just trying to sneak into the Vatican archives."

"Oh no," she gasped, hands to her chest in theatrical panic. "You've caught me. My evil plan is ruined."

His lips twitched, but he didn't laugh. Not exactly.

"You take yourself too seriously," she said. "Do you rehearse that broody face in the mirror?"

He was about to retort when she went silent, her teasing evaporating. Something in her eyes had shifted. She was really thinking. About trust. About risk. There were reasons not to let him in. So many. But something in her chest whispered that maybe she could.

He noticed the stillness and raised an eyebrow. "How come you've stopped talking? Is the universe collapsing?"

Snapped from her thoughts, she narrowed her eyes and smirked. "Fine. I'll take your help. But there are rules. Always two hands away. No flirting. No sudden poetic stares. I'm not one of those girls like Cally and Sasha who drool whenever you breathe."

Caelum turned his head, glancing back over his shoulder. "You already know their names?"

"I overheard them whispering. And swooning. For four days straight."

He shrugged, vaguely impressed. "Hmm."

She gave him a look.

He leaned in, mock seriously. "Let's make something clear, Miss Pea-Head. I don't like chatty girls. Especially the beautiful ones."

Maaya froze, her lips twitching. "Wait, did you just admit I'm beautiful?"

He rolled his eyes. "That's not what I said."

She leaned closer, eyes dancing. *"Aga bai!"* (my goodness in Marathi) she exclaimed, clapping her hands together like a child at mischief. "And yet you said?"

He muttered under his breath, "Nuts."

And just like that, they slipped into a strange new rhythm. Their meetings no longer felt accidental. Their days began with research not love. Not fate. Not yet.

Lucerne Historical Archives became their starting point, where their fingertips had first brushed over a brittle star map. From there, Caelum led her to places tourists never thought to look.

At the **Central and University Library of Lucerne (ZHB Luzern)**, they sat for hours, hidden in the quiet corners of special collections, thumbing through medieval texts and old astronomical records. She struggled with old German. He translated grudgingly but always completely. Then to the

Jesuit Church Library, behind the white-walled beauty by the Reuss River, where parchment whispered in Latin and dust held centuries of forgotten debates on time and the divine.

One mist-cloaked afternoon, they took the train to the **Abbey Library of Saint Gall**. The moment she stepped into the gilded silence beneath its frescoed ceilings, Maaya whispered, "I feel like I've stepped into a memory older than the stars."

Caelum looked at her. Just looked. As if the words had peeled back something in him, he didn't know he was hiding.

One evening, while waiting out the cold in Café Zeitlos, Maaya confessed, "I miss Pune's street food. The chaos. The oil. The soul."

"Street food here doesn't exactly scream spice," Caelum replied.

But he tried.

First, he took her to **Pastarazzi** near **Hirschengraben**, where they stood on the street eating truffle-stuffed ravioli out of a paper tray.

"This is fancy food pretending to be street food," she said, unimpressed.

He arched his brow. "So are you."

She threw a napkin at him.

Next, **Bam Bou by Thomas**, near the university. She tried Thai curry with rosti, her face flushed and teary from the heat.

"You're sweating," he observed.

"I'm crying," she sniffled. "Because this tastes nothing like *vada pav*, but it still tastes like joy."

After one of their long library visits, snow began to fall light, shy flakes brushing the air like forgotten thoughts. They walked to **Lake Lucerne's promenade**, where the Kapellbrücke glowed under lamp light, casting trembling shadows beneath their feet.

Maaya shivered. "There's something about this place. The time here stretches. Like it's waiting for something."

"You always talk like that?" Caelum asked, voice quieter than usual.

"Only when I feel something's about to change."

He didn't answer. But when he walked away that night, her scent followed him—sweet and musky, wild rose and a trace of vanilla. He wanted her closer than he should. Far closer than he knew.

Their conversations meandered.

Maaya would mock him with fake facts and dramatic reenactments. "So, the Gregorian calendar was invented by Pope Gregory the Fiftieth?"

Caelum groaned. "Thirteenth. You know this."

"Do I? Or am I just doing it for fun?"

"You don't need to try so hard. It comes naturally."

But beneath the jokes, real things emerged.

She told him about her mother's love for dance, her father's obsession with calendar theory, and her grandfather, whose eyes had always held galaxies. And she mentioned her own strange memories, some not quite hers. Caelum shared too. His grandfather, once a scientist. His father, a poet. His mother, who left when he was five. "My grandfather believed time was broken," he said softly. "And that it could be rewound."

But neither of them shared everything. Not yet.

One rainy evening, when she mentioned she was staying far away in a hotel, Caelum stiffened.

"You shouldn't be roaming that late alone."

"I can handle myself."

"I didn't say you couldn't," he replied. "I just said you shouldn't have to."

The next morning, without warning, he took her to a small hostel in Wesemlin. A cozy little place run by a retired librarian couple. The rooms smelled of lavender and old paper.

"This is safer," he said, almost gruffly. "And closer to town."

She didn't argue. She just looked at him, then smiled.

But something in him was shifting. Quietly. Surely.

It hit him one evening while walking out of a **fondue bar in Löwengraben**. A man rose from a nearby table as they passed. His eyes lingered on Maaya too long, hungry, intrusive. And then, brushing past, his hand grazed her scarf. Intentional. Ugly.

Caelum stopped mid-step. His body tensed. Storm-grey eyes turned glacial. He stared no, *warned* until the man looked away.

Maaya laughed, unaware. "Was he drunk?"

Caelum didn't answer. But as they walked back that night, he stayed closer. Just close enough.

Maaya, despite the whirlwind of maps, archives, and cold stares, was undeniably intrigued by Caelum. Fascinated, even. There was something about the way he carried the weight of the world in silence as if time itself had stitched secrets into the lines of his jaw.

And it went without saying he was infuriatingly good-looking. The kind of handsome that made heads turn, but he walked past it like it meant nothing. And he never approached Maaya like other Men did. He was calm and composed. And never too much.

If Aanya and Ravi had been there, they would've had a field day.

Aanya, always the romantic, would've clasped her hands dramatically and whispered, "Maaya, he looks like the villain in a dark academia novel but the one you fall for anyway. Look at those eyes! Those are brooding, trauma-rich, emotionally unavailable eyes. My type."

Ravi, on the other hand, would've rolled his eyes and muttered behind his coffee mug, "Red flag with legs. A walking thesis on repressed emotion. Run while you can, Maaya. And for the love of logic, don't fall for the cheekbones."

And would have started singing,

"Do dil mil rahe hai, Magar chupke chupke"

(Two hearts meeting but secretly, Hindi song).

Maaya smiled at the thought, chewing the inside of her cheek.

Yes, Maaya is a bit bossy. Maybe more than *a bit*. She had the annoying habit of always believing she was right. But that didn't stop her from purposefully poking Caelum's patience every now and then mocking his brooding intensity, teasing his obsession with control. She knew exactly how to get under his skin, and she did it often. Not out of malice, but because well, when he got flustered, or slightly angry, or rolled his eyes in exhausted defeat it made him talk more. And when he talked more, she got to stay longer.

And truth be told, she liked that time. A little too much. But even with their voices echoing in her head, she couldn't shake the way her heart had started keeping a separate rhythm; one that only played when Caelum was nearby.

It was foolish. Ridiculous. Probably dangerous.

But she was Maaya. And danger, after all, had never looked so intriguing.

Another time outside the **Lucerne City Wall (Museggmauer)**, Maaya slipped on the icy stone steps while photographing the Zyt Tower. He caught her before she fell his hand steady at her elbow.

They froze. Her breath, a cloud against his collarbone.

"You can let go now," she said, voice barely above a whisper.

"I know," he murmurs.

But he didn't. Not for a moment longer.

Shadows Beneath the Clocktower

The days had turned intense. Their search was no longer confined to libraries and manuscripts. They scoured ancient research papers, chased footnotes that led to dusty margins of forgotten journals, spoke to old professors tucked away in universities, and even knocked on the doors of eccentric historians. They stopped anyone who might carry a whisper of truth.

And when logic failed them, they crossed into intuition consulting astrologers in quiet corners of Lucerne, decoding planetary charts, sitting across old women with crystal pendants and strange maps who spoke of alignments and echoes of time. Maaya believed every lead was a thread, and Caelum, half-curious and half-drawn by her madness, followed.

But today, the madness had a price.

They were seated at their usual corner table at the quiet café near Helvetiaplatz, the sky outside growing dusky, their table cluttered with scribbled notes, printouts, and two steaming mugs. Maaya was unusually cheerful, despite the long day they'd had chasing dead ends.

Caelum, hunched over a translated document from the **Jesuit** archives, had barely spoken for twenty minutes. His brows were furrowed in concentration, lips tight, jaw working the inside of his cheek as he annotated with near-military precision.

Maaya watched him, arms folded across her chest.

"You know," she said, breaking the silence, "if you stare any harder at that paper, it might file a harassment complaint."

He didn't look up. "This document holds a very specific clue. Your incessant commentary doesn't."

"Oof." She leaned in, lowering her voice dramatically. "And here I was, thinking we were having a charming moment."

"Then I'd hate to see your version of a tragic one."

She gasped, hand to chest, mock-offended. "Wow. You've been practicing. That was almost funny. Almost."

Still no smile from him. He scribbled another note in the margin.

Maaya rolled her eyes and picked up her spoon, stirring her tea like it was a potion.

"Oh, come on," she chuckled, twirling the spoon with theatrical flair. "You're so uptight, Caelum. You probably alphabetize your nightmares."

She leaned back, balancing her chair on two legs with the confidence of a girl who'd never had to regret falling.

"I swear, the madness must be hereditary — just like mother, like son!"

She laughed. Loudly. **Too** loudly.

The kind of laugh that wasn't just laughter, but an explosion unfiltered, carefree, a little mean without meaning to be. It broke the stillness of the café like a wrong chord struck hard in a quiet concert hall. Her shoulders shook with amusement she hadn't tried to check.

But Caelum wasn't laughing.

He didn't move. Didn't blink. Didn't twitch. He just *stared* at her.

He looked up. His voice, when it came, was cold. Icy. Controlled.

"What did you just say?"

Maaya's smile faltered. "It was a joke, Caelum. Don't be so"

"No," he cut in, his voice sharper now, trembling just beneath the surface. "Say it again. Say it like you meant it."

"Caelum, I didn't mean"

But he stood abruptly, his chair scraping back. "You know what your problem is?" His voice rose. "You cross lines, always. Then hide behind your smart mouth."

Maaya blinked, taken aback. "It was just a joke. Why are you?"

"I'm done pretending this is all fun and quirky," he snapped. "You're acting like a madwoman. Obsessing over every stone, every shadow. What exactly are you searching for, Maaya? Huh?"

He pointed to the piles of notes. "Every day we chase ghosts. Astrologers. Random strangers. You burst out at me, insult me, mock me like I'm just a tool for your wild chase. At the end of the day, this is just research! Why are you making it your entire existence?"

Maaya swallowed hard. "Because it matters."

"To *you*, maybe!" he shouted now. "And maybe I get that it could be a big breakthrough in temporal physics. Sure. Maybe it changes things. But you"

He paused, his breath ragged. "You know what I think?"

Maaya didn't respond. Her eyes searched for him, already glistening.

"I think you're hungry for fame," he spat. "You don't care about time or physics or truth. You care about legacy. Your name in the journals. That's all this is."

Her lip trembled, but she looked away.

"I've been selflessly helping you," he said, voice breaking into disbelief. "Running after your riddles. Trying to understand your tantrums. Taking your insults. All because I thought maybe you were alone in a new country and needed someone."

He shook his head. "But now? Now I see something's *wrong* with you. Seriously wrong. What are you hiding? Tell me."

Maaya opened her mouth to speak but no words came. Her throat burned.

He took a step forward. "Tell me."

She finally said, soft and shaky, "You don't know what's in my mind"

"Because you won't let me!" he shouted.

She stood up. “Please stop getting hyper, please, Caelum, please”

“Then tell me!” he roared.

And then, like a crack tearing open the earth, her voice broke through

“Yes! I have an intention!”

He froze.

“Yes,” she repeated, louder this time, tears spilling now. “I have an intention. But not the one you think. Not evil. Not selfish. And *not* for fame.”

He stared at her, silent. Breathing hard.

She inhaled sharply, her chest heaving. And finally, she let it go.

“I came here to find my father.” He is long lost. Our entire family has shattered after my father vanished. My Mother became a living dead; my grandfather died with an untold ache in heart for his lost son.

The world fell still.

“And those pairs of silver eyes” she whispered, “a pair of silver eyes I saw in a dream. Eyes that looked just like yours.”

Her voice cracked, almost childlike now. “I thought it was just a dream at first. But then the pieces started to fit. Clocks. Maps. Names. Whispers of things I was never told but somehow… remembered. And then”

She stopped, choking back a sob.

"And then I saw *you*."

Caelum's throat tightened. "Maaya"

But she pulled back.

"Notice how you went for me," she said bitterly, "how you tore me down, how you assumed the worst. But not once did you stop and ask why I looked like I was breaking."

Tears slipped down her cheeks in silence now. Her voice barely whispers.

"You think I'm childish? I'm trying not to drown."

Caelum stood there, heart pounding, every word she said sinking in like rain through stone. He felt his anger crumble. Guilt rushed in like a wave.

Maaya took a breath, wiped her tears, and sat down exhausted.

"Don't pity me," she murmured. "Just don't."

The candle on the table flickered in the draft. Papers rustled softly.

And for the first time since they met, neither of them had anything left to say.

After the explosion, after the storm of words and wounds, Maaya was gone. She had thrown the notes across the cobblestone like dead leaves in the wind papers that once meant everything to her, now fluttering like white flags of surrender under a dusky sky.

She didn't pick up calls.
Didn't respond to messages.
Didn't exist, for an entire day.

Caelum searched through the city, through the noise in his head, retracing every alley, every tram stop, every place they had laughed or argued or simply *been*. His mind raced with possibilities, each one darker than the last.

And then near 11 p.m., in a side street off **Helvetiaplatz** where the city thinned into quiet, he saw her.

She was leaning against the cold stone edge of a dry, forgotten fountain. A bottle of cheap liquor dangled from her hand. Her hair tangled in the night wind. Her eyes are glassy, far away. And around her, shadows moved three men, circling like vultures. Drunk. Smirking. Closing in.

The next few seconds unraveled like fire through dry grass.

A flash of movement.
A fist across a jaw.
A **grunt**.
Someone hit the ground.
Another **lunged**.

Caelum didn't feel the pain, only rage, only fear. One man screamed as his wrist cracked under Caelum's grip. Then silence.

Breathing hard, bleeding slightly, he turned to her.

She looked at him with blurred eyes. Her lips trembled not from cold, but from something that had broken deeper.

"I ruined everything," she whispered.

He didn't answer.

He just lifted her into his arms.

He carried her to the nearest hotel, just off the quiet corner of the Reuss river. The night outside howled against the windows, but the room was still warm, cocooned in soft orange lamplight and the faint hum of silence.

He laid her down on the bed gently, like she was made of memory. Her breath was uneven, stained with wine and sorrow.

"You didn't have to come," she murmured, eyes barely open.

Caelum stood there, hands clenched at his sides. "You think I had a choice?"

Maaya's fingers reached for him weak but wanting.

For a moment, nothing moved between them just breath and grief and a pull neither of them understood. Her eyes shimmered, glassy pools of hurt and heat, and his heart broke watching her.

There was something about the way she looked at him right then like he was both punishment and mercy.

Like her pain had finally found a place to rest.

He knelt beside the bed, brushed the back of her hand with his lips.

"Don't ever do that again," he whispered, voice barely audible. "Don't disappear like that. Not from me."

She blinked slowly. "Why?"

"Because" he exhaled, voice cracking, "it felt like the sky fell in."

She leaned forward, just a little. "Then hold me, before it falls again."

And then they kissed.

It wasn't gentle.
It wasn't polite.
It was a storm of everything unspoken. Of heartbreak and hunger and everything they'd kept dammed up behind reason. Her hands curled into his shirt, pulling him closer like she could press the pain out of her chest through his heartbeat.

But then he stopped.

Breathless, he pulled away, forehead resting against hers, eyes shut.

"Maaya," he said, voice trembling, "you're not sober."

She tried to argue. "I'm fine."

"No," he whispered, his voice cracking. "No, I won't touch you like this. Not like this. Don't test my patience Maaya."

She stared at him, confused, aching.

"I respect you too much to let this become a mistake you wake up regretting."

And then, with the quietest heartbreak, he brushed her hair off her cheek, tucked her beneath the blanket, and pulled it up over her shoulder.

She closed her eyes. A single tear slipped down the curve of her temple.

He didn't leave.
He turned off the lights.
Then walked across the room and sat on the couch, his head in his hands.

But he didn't sleep. Not yet.

He watched from across the room, where the golden lamplight brushed softly over the gentle slope of her face and the curve of one bare shoulder. Inky waves of hair spilled across the pillow wild, untamed, like the girl who had just unraveled him. Lips slightly parted still seemed to carry the taste of everything left unsaid.

Her breathing had steadied slow, delicate, like petals falling. The blanket had slipped down just enough to reveal the smooth line of her collarbone and the soft dip beneath it, a delicate trace of cleavage rising and falling with each unguarded breath. That same rhythm moved through the outline of her waist, quiet and steady, as if the universe had chosen this moment to pause and admire its own creation.

Curled gently into the bed, her hourglass form melted into the sheets, the curve of her waist disappearing into the soft outline of her hips. Skin flushed from the cold, and wine glowed with a warmth that stirred something deep within him, an ache he couldn't name, a gravity he couldn't resist. She lay completely unaware, undone by exhaustion and heartache yet still devastatingly beautiful in her most fragile, human form.

His eyes lingered not out of disrespect, but reverence. Desire crept in softly, like a confession. She was *dangerous* in that moment not because of how she looked, but because of what she had unknowingly carved into him.

A part of him wanted to reach for her. To bury his face in her neck, to whisper all the things he hadn't said. But he didn't. He just watched. And in his mind, words came uninvited, like verses slipping through the cracks of his restraint.

"She burns like wine in veins of frost,
A storm wrapped up in skin and gloss,
Her silence louder than the stars,
My ruin wears her name like scars."

He smiled faintly.
A real smile.
God, he was becoming his father. A poet in love with a storm.

And with that thought nestled somewhere between his ribs, he leaned back on the couch. His gaze still fixed on her.

And then slowly, quietly he fell asleep.

She woke with a headache and a storm twisting inside her.

The unfamiliar ceiling above her spun slightly before coming into focus, bathed in the soft gold glow of morning light spilling through gauzy curtains. Her mouth was dry, her temples pounding, and yet it wasn't the hangover that unnerved her. It was the hollow in her chest, the weight of not remembering everything.

Then she saw him. Caelum.

Sitting by the window, still in the same clothes from last night, a half-empty glass of water in his hand, eyes puffy from lack of sleep. He looked like he'd been guarding her all night watching time pass like it was something sacred.

She slowly sat up, pulling the blanket tighter around her.

Her voice came out cracked, fragile. "Why are you here? What happened last night?"

He looked at her with that same unreadable face, but his eyes were soft, like dusk after a storm.

"You cried," he said simply. "Then tried to seduce me."

Her eyes widened. "I what?!"

He didn't flinch. Just raised an eyebrow, far too calm. "You were dramatic. Tearful. Call me your emotional anchor or something equally poetic. And then you kissed me."

She flushed deeply. "I did *not*!"

A beat.

"Relax," he said dryly, leaning back into the chair. "You failed. Miserably."

She grabbed a pillow and threw it at him with the last ounce of dignity she had. "You're insufferable!"

The pillow bounced off his chest. And for the first time not a smirk, not a condescending quirk of his lips but a full laugh burst from Caelum. Unfiltered. Careless. Like the sound had been locked inside him for years.

It filled the room.

Maaya blinked, stunned not by the sound, but by how human it made him look. How heartbreakingly beautiful.

"God," she whispered without thinking, "you look different when you laugh."

He stilled, the last of his chuckle hanging in the air between them. His smile faded, softened into something quieter. Something that looked a lot like surrender.

And in that moment, something shifted. Not just in the room.

But in them.

Later that day, back at her hostel, Maaya lay on her bed, bathed in the soft pink-orange hue of late afternoon sunlight streaming through the window. She was still reeling from the morning from the fragments of warmth, of something almost like love, that had curled around her heart and refused to let go.

She smiled. Without reason. Without logic. The pain that had clouded her for days, her search, her obsession, her father, the clock ticking endlessly behind her thoughts all of it blurred into a quiet hum. Because now, she could only think of him.

Caelum.

His voice. His hands. His restraint. Had she really kissed him?

Why couldn't she remember it clearly? Her mind was a haze like the moment had existed only in smoke. And yet, her lips remembered. Her heart remembered. And somewhere deep inside her, the memory burned like a forbidden echo she'd never be able to hold in her hands. Her cheeks flushed.

What is happening to me?

In a sudden burst of impulsive emotion, she pulled out her phone and started playing old Hindi romantic tracks, the ones she hadn't heard in years, the ones her heart always responded to like it had a secret it couldn't tell.

Her voice joined the melody softly at first and then louder, fuller, dancing barefoot across the wooden floor, her dupatta catching air like a swirl of color:

"Usne baat ki kuch aise dhang se,
Sapne de gaya hazaaron rang ke…
Rah jaaun jaise main haar ke…
Aur choome vo mujhe pyaar se…
Pehla nasha…"

(He spoke in such a way,
That he left me with dreams of a thousand hues…
As if I surrendered, defeated…
And then he kissed me with love…
First intoxication… **Hindi song)**

She spun once, eyes closed. She was floating. A girl in love, or maybe something dangerously close to it.

But then the pop of a notification tone. It sliced through the air like a needle through silk.

She froze mid-step, her dupatta falling from her shoulder.

Her heart quickened. It must be Caelum. She lunged toward the bed where her phone rested. Unlocked it.

But it wasn't him.

An email. From a private address. No subject. No reply option.

She frowned. Her breath slowed. Curious. Suspicious. Almost afraid and yet unable to stop herself she tapped.

And read:

"To unlock the past you never knew,
Come alone, the answers wait for you."

Below it: a single location pin.

Her blood ran cold.

She called Caelum. Once. Twice. Three times. No answer.

She sent a message. Attached the address. Then stood there, fingers shaking, heart pounding.

She should wait. But she didn't.

∞

Chapter Four:
When the Past Sends for You

∞

The path to its domain was older than memory worn thin by centuries of forgotten footsteps. It wound like a scar through the forest, narrow and uneven, each stone and root jutting upward as if trying to catch her. The air thickened with every step Maaya took, clinging cold to her skin, a damp, breathless chill as though the forest itself exhaled frost in slow, deliberate sighs.

Shadows gathered where they should have broken apart, shifting in strange, liquid ways bending, recoiling, and stretching without a whisper of wind.

The silence was wrong.
Not peaceful oppressive.
The kind that presses against the eardrums until they ache.
Even the birds had abandoned this place, as if the branches themselves forbade their song.

Her GPS flickered once then went black. No signal. No time. Just an inert slab of glass and steel in her hand, useless as a stone.

Maaya stood frozen on the dirt path, her breath coiling into the air, her pulse hammering a hollow, ancient rhythm she didn't recognize but felt she had always known. A cold instinct, buried deep in her bones, screamed to turn back.

Then—

Crunch.

From behind her, dry leaves broke under deliberate weight.

A man stepped out from between the skeletal trees. He was so thin it was hard to tell where flesh ended and shadow began. His skin was pale to the point of translucence, veins whispering faintly beneath the surface like blue cracks in porcelain. The long brown coat that clung to him was two sizes too large, the sleeves swallowing his hands, the hem trailing in the leaves.

His face was a perfect mask, lips pressed into a colorless line, jaw set like carved stone. But it was his eyes that arrested her vast, black, and depthless, holding neither warmth nor malice. Just… an absence.

And the way he moved
Slow. Careful.
Like a marionette that had been taught, long ago, how to mimic human movement… and had never quite mastered it.

"Miss Maaya?" he asked.

She nodded cautiously.

"I've been sent to collect you."

"By whom?"

"You'll see," he said, voice low, metallic.

Her instincts screamed. Every ounce of logic told her to run. But the past had dangled itself just close enough to touch, and something inside her stubborn, desperate overruled fear.

She climbed into the coughing, rust-covered lorry.

They drove without speaking.

The trees thickened. Arched overhead like bones. The road narrowed until it became a trail. Branches clawed at the windows. Time stretched.

In the middle of no where

"Where is this place?" Maaya asked with a broken voice. No reply came back.

And then the gate. Iron. Old. Covered in moss and secrets. It groaned as it opened.

Beyond it, a house no, a structure that remembered being a house. Stone crumbling. Windows broken. A nameplate so eroded it was unreadable. It didn't just look abandoned. It looked haunted by its own past.

The man led her inside. A long corridor. Wood creaking beneath her feet. Dust swimming in narrow shafts of light. He opened the door. A small wooden room. No windows.

Sparse. Cold. A table. A single chair.
A tray with stale sandwiches and a cup of coffee long gone cold.

"Wait here," he said.

Then locked the door.

The sound of the lock clicking echoed in her spine. She lunged for the handle.

Banged on the door.
"HEY! LET ME OUT! LET ME OUT! PLEASE, PLEASE!"

Silence. Utter silence.

"Caelum…" she whispered, voice trembling. "Where are you…"

She slid down to the floor, tears slipping down her cheeks. Her throat tightened. Panic clawed at her. Her body shook with adrenaline.

And then, something inside her shifted. She wiped her face. Stood up. Her eyes scanned the room. If they brought her here, they wanted something.

There was an old desk, shoved into the corner. She approached it slowly. One drawer. Rusted handle. Locked. She pulled. It resisted. Then gave way with a groan.

Inside:

Yellowed pages. Equations. Planetary sketches. Celestial harmonics. Gregorian correction patterns. Notes written in faded ink. A black-and-white photograph: eight men in coats, standing before a building.

At the bottom, in elegant cursive:
Ordo Aevi Éternum.

She turned the photo. Two names written on the back.

Leon Weiss. Leonhardt Virek.

She gasped.

That name Leon Weiss. She'd seen it in the margins of her father's notebooks.

Beside it sat an old Parker Vacumatic fountain pen. 1940s.

She reached for it slowly. Held it in her palm.

It was identical to the one her grandfather used to sign her birthday cards.
The same nick on the cap. The same gold trim.

Maaya's knees gave way. She sat on the floor, breath trembling. This wasn't a coincidence. This wasn't madness. She hadn't just been chasing the past.

The past had reached out, wrapped its fingers around her throat. And locked her inside.

Enchanted Beyond the Archives

Caelum had spent the entire afternoon buried in the dim corners of the university archives, surrounded by brittle manuscripts and time-worn theories that should have offered him solace. Yet the only fire that consumed his thoughts was her. He marveled at how completely she had enchanted his mind, how a man so solemn by nature now found himself smiling too easily and speaking far more than he ever had before.

Maaya.

Her name alone stirred the storm.

He stared at the faded parchment in front of him but couldn't see a word. The world around him had dulled to a shadow, the only sound echoing in his mind was her voice, her laugh, the way she threw sarcasm like confetti, her maddening way of talking too much and yet never quite revealing enough.

Caelum clenched his jaw, burying his head in his hands.

What was this madness? Why couldn't he escape her?

"It's just infatuation, Caelum," he muttered to himself like a fool.

"Just physical attraction. It'll pass. She's beautiful God, too beautiful but it's nothing more than that."

But the lie shattered even before it reached the edge of his lips. Because it wasn't just her beauty. It was the way her voice lingered like warmth long after she left the room. It was the strange way her energy filled the space as though the molecules themselves turned toward her.

And it was the eyes. Those violet eyes. It's unique, it's just rare for an Indian girl.

Eyes he had seen in his own dreams, long before she walked into his life.

That violet glow, floating in darkness like a memory from another lifetime. When she confessed yesterday out of nowhere, in a fit of rage that she saw a pair of silver eyes from a dream and those eyes had matched his, *he* had frozen. And buried it.

Because she was already drowning in pain. And he couldn't pour another weight into her.

But now that buried truth was boiling to the surface.

He had sat there for hours in silence, the pages untouched, time ticking meaninglessly past him. Until a hard shove to his shoulder.

"Wanna grab a coffee, daydreamer?" Markus smirked, holding two steaming cups and raising a brow.

Caelum blinked back into the present like a man surfacing from a deep, dark lake. He rubbed his eyes.

"No. I have to rush," he said hastily, standing. "Some other day. Thank you." And then

He smiled.

A small, real, ungritted smile.

Markus stood frozen as Caelum walked away.

"He smiled?" he muttered to himself. "What on *earth* happened to that grumpy marble statue?"

Back at his small flat, Caelum threw his coat over the chair and headed for the kitchen until he spotted it.

His phone. Lying face-down on the coffee table. Silent.

He picked it up, unlocked it casually then froze.

Missed calls. Maaya's name. Again. And again.

A pit opened in his chest. Cold, gnawing.

He called her back. No answer. Called again. Voicemail.

He ran a hand through his hair, pacing now.

"Maaya… where the hell are you?"

His voice cracked quietly, fractured, like glass under pressure.

"I swear, if you've done anything reckless again"

He paused.

"I'm going to strangle you myself," he said, voice breaking into a whisper. "And then wrap you in a blanket and never let you out of my sight."

The kind of crack that splits a man into a thousand silent pieces.

Then a chime. A notification.

Markus.

"What happened to you, Caelum? You smiled at me today"

Caelum barely registered it.

And then he saw it.

A cryptic message from Maaya. Sent hours ago.

No explanation. Just an address.

A pin-drop. On the edge of the Swiss Alps.

No reply. No follow-up.

And in that moment, something inside him ruptured.

Caelum had never feared anything in his life. Not the dark. Not the unknown. Not even death.

But today he felt fear clawing through his chest like a wild animal. Fear for her.

For that violet-eyed girl who mocked him, challenged him, enchanted him, and shook the very foundation of everything he believed.

He grabbed his coat. And ran. Out of the door. Into the wind. Into the dusk that now bled across the city like spilled ink.

And as the sky turned copper above Lucerne, and shadows stretched long over the trembling lake, Caelum's mind echoed only one thing-

"Please be safe, Maaya Please"

Because her silence had begun to rattle inside his chest like loose bolts in a breaking machine.

And by nightfall, that rattling had turned to dread.

And The Search Begins

Maaya sat cross-legged on the dusty wooden floor, her breath slowing, the pen still cradled in her hand like a relic. Her mind buzzed with half-memories whispers from childhood, the smell of ink and old parchment, the ticking of her grandfather's study clock.

How did this pen come here? Why here?

She placed it gently beside the photograph and turned to the pile of documents, pages upon pages of handwritten calculations, diagrams, phrases written in Latin and German and sometimes Sanskrit.

"**Devikalāna**" she whispered, seeing the word underlined in red.

Her father's notes used that term '**the divine chronology'** the moment time bends toward change.

Her fingers moved faster now, desperate to stitch together meaning from fragments. Symbols began to match. Numbers echoed. A name. A place. An alignment date.

Then a creak outside the door. Footsteps. Heavy. Slow. She stood instantly, heartbeat hammering. The handle jiggled. Then stopped.

Silence.

Maaya backed up to the far end of the room, her breath shallow.
Maaya's mind raced. She picked up the pen again not for writing, but to hold, to wield like a dagger if she had to.

The door clicked. Swung open.

But no one entered. Just a breath of cold air.

Then a voice low, male, steady. Familiar.

"You shouldn't have come alone, Maaya."

She froze. The voice wasn't one she'd heard in years.

She stepped forward slowly, the darkness of the hallway yawning like an open mouth.

"Baba?"

Caelum stood on the gravel path at the edge of the woods, hands clenched, breath visible in the cold night air. He'd followed the location she sent him until the map failed, then his instincts took over.

And now he was standing before a rusted iron gate that moaned with the weight of time.

Beyond it nothing. No sound. No sign of life. Just a haunting silence that felt too thick to breathe through.

But there was one thing he knew for certain.

She was there.

And if something had happened to her, he didn't finish the thought. He simply climbed the gate.

Caelum found the front door pried half-open, its hinges rotted. He stepped inside cautiously, flashlight in hand. Every wall bore the scent of mildew and secrets. The deeper he went, the louder his pulse became.

He didn't call her name. Not yet. He didn't want to alert anyone else.

Maaya followed the voice down a long hallway, lit only by flickering bulbs and shafts of moonlight through broken shutters. Every part of her screamed to run but that voice, her father's voice, tugged her like gravity.

Then she entered the room. No one.

Just a dusty chair. A reel projector sitting idle. And a large circular mirror on the wall, like an ancient clock face, its edge engraved with zodiac signs.

Suddenly, the projector flickered to life on its own.

The reel spun. Maaya stepped back.

A man appeared on the wall. Black-and-white. Faintly glitching.

Her father.

Alive. Speaking.

"Maaya, if you're seeing this, it means time has bent exactly as I feared it would"

Her legs gave out beneath her.

"You must not trust them. Not all of them. There are doors that were never meant to open."

Suddenly, a hand clamped over her mouth from behind.

She screamed into the silence.

Caelum heard the muffled cry echo from deep within the house.

His heart stopped.

Then surged.

He ran faster than he thought he could through halls, down stairwells, kicking open doors, shouting her name now

"MAAYA!"

He burst through a corridor at the back of the mansion, following instinct, sound, memory, her.

Then he found the room. He found her.

Thrown against the projector, struggling. A man in a dark coat looming over her.

Caelum didn't hesitate. He crashed into the man, dragging him off her, fists flying, rage unleashed.

When the silence returned, the man was out cold. Caelum's hands trembled as he reached for her face.

"Maaya are you okay?"

She couldn't speak. She just nodded. Then grabbed him and held him like she would never let go.

She finally whispered:

"I think this place is where it all began but it's not where it ends."

Maaya was trembling in his arms.

Caelum cradled her gently, one hand stroking her hair, the other still bloodied from the fight. The old reel behind them had stopped spinning, leaving only a dim crackling light that played across their exhausted faces.

"It's over," he whispered, voice hoarse. "I'm here now. Nothing will happen to you."

Maaya clung to him like a lifeline, her body still shaking, tears warm against his shirt. "I was so scared. I thought I'd never see you again."

He pressed a kiss to her forehead, slow and grounding. "I've got you. I promise."

And then.

A loud metallic THUD.

It echoed through the room like a cannon blast.

Caelum barely had time to turn.

Crack.

A sickening sound, something heavy slamming against the back of his skull.

His body jerked violently.

Maaya screamed.

"Caelum!"

He collapsed to the floor in front of her limp, breath shallow, eyes rolling back.

Maaya's voice turned to a frantic wail.

"Caelum No wake up! Wake up, darling, please!" She dropped to her knees, shaking him, sobbing,

"Please open your eyes! What happened?! Please don't do this to me, Caelum don't leave me"

And then a deep, guttural laugh.

Low. Sinister. Echoing off every wall like it came from the house itself.

Maaya froze.

The laugh got louder. Crueler.

She turned.

But there was no one.

Not yet.

Caelum, in his unconsciousness, was drifting not into blackness, but into memory. His mind spun, pulling him down a tunnel of flickering images and sounds. He wasn't awake but he wasn't fully gone either.

And in that liminal space between reality and dream, he saw a face emerge from the shadows.

A man. Tall. Striking. Familiar. Too familiar. But older. Hollowed. And impossibly alive.

The laughter echoed again, this time right in front of him.

Caelum tried to move, to speak, but his limbs wouldn't obey. His vision darkened at the edges, his heart hammering.

The man leaned closer.

"Still too soft," he sneered. "Still playing protector, just like your mother wanted."

Caelum's lips parted in disbelief. His pupils dilated.

"No, it can't be"

But it was. The face, the voice, the man who raised him in stories and poems, the man who was buried years ago.

His father.

Now standing there, in the shadows, laughing at him like death itself had forgotten to finish the job.

Caelum's breath caught in his throat. And then darkness.

Total, crushing blackness.

∞

Chapter Five: Kālachakra Disrupted

∞

(The Wheel of Time, Unbound)

By the mid-1940s, Switzerland stood at a strange crossroads outwardly calm, inwardly trembling. The war howled beyond its borders, yet within, everything was suspended in a tense, crystalline quiet. The cafés of Zurich spoke in code; letters vanished between Bern and Berlin; the gold flowing through Geneva's vaults gleamed a little too darkly. Even the air over the Alps felt watchful, Allied and Axis planes crossed the borders with uncanny precision, and the neutral mountains seemed to listen more than they echoed.

It was in those years, between the dying winter of 1940 and the uneasy dawn of 1941, that the first irregularities were noticed, clocks losing minutes only to regain them hours later, mountain shadows shifting before the sun, water freezing in patterns that looked almost like script. Officially, the phenomena were dismissed as illusions of war weariness. Unofficially, they were not ignored.

In the hollowed ribs of the Swiss Alps, where light thins and silence calcifies into stone, something breathes that should not. Beneath the icy black waters of **Lac Souterrain**, hidden from all known topographies, exists an order whose very name is a paradox: **Ordo Aevi Éternum — "The Order of Eternal Time."** The name itself is a construct of Latin illusion, coined by exiled astronomer-priests in 1613 who believed that time, like serpents in winter, coils back upon itself.

The Order's work had resumed under the guise of "scientific

continuity experiments." In abandoned railway tunnels near Sion and shuttered observatories near Monthey, they gathered physicists, priests, and soldiers turned scholars drawn by the same anomaly: time had begun to hesitate. And somewhere beneath the mountains, in chambers older than maps, they swore to measure not the passing of hours, but the folding of them.

The society's emblem was a cipher in ink and stone. A serpent consuming its own tail, entwined around a broken astrolabe. **Eternitas fracta avaritia**. Eternity fractured by greed. This was not a brotherhood of religion, but of rhythm. These were men who decoded time not as linear progression but as recursion, symmetry, recurrence. They believed the Gregorian calendar was not a tool of timekeeping, but a map of celestial harmonics, a blueprint that hid rare "echo years," such as **1941 and 2025**, whose identical calendar structures mirrored deeper cosmic truths.

$$\mathbf{g(t) \approx g\,(t + nY)}$$

(Where 'g' is the Gregorian sequence, 't' is the temporal year, and 'nY' is any echo interval divisible by 28 or 84 planetary resonance cycles.)

Such years, they believed, were not arbitrary recurrences. They were gateways. Temporal soft spots. Points where **kāla** the Sanskrit word for time thinned like stretched parchment, and where the past and future did not flow, but folded.

For centuries, Ordo Aevi Éternum pursued these patterns through Newton's laws, then Einstein's relativity. But something never clicked. The math was precise. The sky is compliant. Yet time refused to open. What they lacked, they soon discovered, was not logic. It was longing. The variable was not hidden in the stars but in the heart. In Sanskrit, the word for memory is **Smṛti**. And **Smṛti**, like gravity, had weight.

Then came a whisper, not from the sky, but stone. A reference fragment. A scribbled glyph in a forgotten codex unearthed from their deepest vault a glyph that led not to Europe, but to the veiled east. Beyond cartography. Beyond names.

It led to **Pemakö**, the mythic "hidden lotus" of Tibet, and within it, a monastery so carefully erased from memory it had become legend **Tsal'Kar**.

In the old Tibetan tongue, *Tsal* means essence, and *Kar* means cycle. The Cycle of Essence. Tsal'Kar was not merely a monastery. It was a seal. A hinge in the hidden mechanism of time.

Here, monks followed what they called the **Samaya-Vaartal** (the Vow of Temporal Accord). In Sanskrit, *samaya* means sacred agreement or union, and *vaartal* refers to flow or exchange. This was not a religion. It was the physics of devotion. A science of soul. They did not measure time in minutes but in resonance, tracking how love, loss, and memory echoed across generations. The Gregorian calendar, they believed, occasionally aligned with rare planetary harmonics to form **Rituchakra Sannivesh (**seasonal-wheel alignments) when years like 1941 and 2025 mirrored not just date structures, but entire karmic blueprints.

Time, in these moments, could ripple.

But only when activated by human emotion.

Machines could not do it. Calculations could not compel it. The force required was trifold **prema** (love), **smṛti** (memory), and **raktavāṁśa** (bloodline). These three formed the foundational triad of what the Ordo would later call Resonance Convergence. A theory not of time travel, but of time resonance where aligned emotions anchored in matching years could thin the veil and create folds. Folds that did not jump, but mirrored, reset, and looped.

The monks of Tsal'Kar protected this knowledge like fire sealed in clay. They hid it not from malice, but from mercy. Because in the right hands, this wisdom could **heal ancestral trauma**, **reverse ecological collapse**, or **amend historic tragedy** but only at devastating cost. To change time, the monks believed, one must pay with **self-erasure**. One's memory. Or one's love. Only the purest grief could realign the wheel.

In the wrong hands, however, this was not salvation. It was controlled. A loop could become a cage. A fold could become a weapon. Causality could be rewritten, entire bloodlines erased. Season would slip from cycle. The future would cease to exist.

Then came the man who would break the seal.

Leon Weiss..

Leon Weiss was not merely a mathematician. He was a cartographer of time mapping its folds with the cold precision of **chronophysics** and the aching devotion of a man chasing something lost. As a boy, he'd watched his mother die in a sudden accident, her absence becoming the silent force behind every equation he later wrote. Rebecca, a kind librarian, had adopted him soon after, giving him love, safety, and books but never the one thing he still longed for a way back.

Though he spoke only of theory, Leonhardt Virek, his closest confidant, understood the truth that Weiss's obsession with time wasn't academic. It was personal. He wanted to return. To change one moment. To save her. He was haunted not by wonder, but by need. Weiss found Tsal'Kar through the alignment of astronomy, arithmetic, and ancient theft. Obsessed with calendar symmetry and mythic physics, he came to the monastery with hunger in his heart. The guardian monk who protected the final scroll offered him no resistance. Only warning. But Weiss could not leave empty-handed.

In the shadow of prayer flags, he killed him.

As the monk collapsed, he whispered, "If time bends without grief… it will not bend. It will break."

Weiss returned to Switzerland with the scroll pressed between blood and ink. He lied to Virek, telling him the monks had offered it freely, impressed by their honesty and discipline. Virek believed him. He did not know yet what unspoken guilt can evolve into ambition carved into obsession.

In the caverns of Ordo Aevi Éternum, Weiss devoured the scroll. It was not written in diagrams, but dreams. Not equations, but echoes. It spoke not of machinery, but of emotional immersion, a sacrifice not of flesh, but of soul-resonance. To enter the fold of time was not to leap through a portal. It was to become the vibration itself. The experiment required not genius, but grief.

And Weiss, by then, had both.

The Folded Echoes of Samvidāna

After retrieving the scroll from Tsal'Kar, Leon Weiss and Leonhardt Virek dedicated themselves to translating its cryptic symbols, aligning Sanskrit riddles with planetary charts, and plotting Gregorian calendar echoes. Over months of sleepless calculations, they uncovered something extraordinary: the year 1941 was not just a mirror to 2025 in structure, but part of an ancient celestial rhythm predicted by both Eastern doctrine and Western math. A rare solstice, planetary harmonics, and calendar symmetry had created a fragile corridor in spacetime, a kāla-jhīla, a time-pond, where memory and matter might ripple forward.

But the scroll was clear: time would not open to intellect alone. The fold could not be breached with equations or machinery. It responded only to emotional resonance, the echoes of grief, love, and memory passed through blood. This was the heart of Resonance Convergence. It required a soul willing to become a bridge.

The decision was not made lightly. Virek, ever the cautious one, proposed simulations. Controlled pulses. But Weiss, burning with guilt over the monk's death and consumed by an ambition that now bordered on sacred mania, insisted. He believed his emotional state was ideal: raw, unresolved, deeply human. He would be the subject.

Beneath the Ordo's glacial vaults, they prepared the chamber. Carved directly into the mountain's bedrock, it was circled with concentric copper rings, inscribed with the planetary seals derived from both the scroll and Einstein's relativistic field equations. The walls bore the glyphs of Samaya-Vaartal, inked in ash and iron. At the center, a copper basin where the offering would be made.

On the night of the Omega Solstice, when the sky matched the scroll's ancient calculations, Weiss stood within the final ring. In his hand, he carried his mother's pendant, wrapped in a letter of guilt he never sent. It would be his smṛti his memory-offering.

The process was simple in theory, but perilous in execution. The chamber was set to resonate with cosmic harmonics during a thirty-two-minute window on the night of the Omega Solstice. The scroll prescribed a precise sequence of chants, planetary invocations, and a final emotional offering, an artifact tied to a personal loss. Weiss carried with him a pendant that once belonged to his mother, wrapped in a letter he never sent. He placed it in the copper basin at the center of the floor.

At the predicted moment, the lights dimmed. The air grew viscous. A low hum began, not from machines, but from the stone itself as though the mountain remembered something. Weiss stepped into the center ring, breathing slowly, repeating the final verse of the scroll in Sanskrit:

"**Yadi kāla smarati, tadā mṛtyu nāsti**."

If time remembers, then death does not exist.

For a heartbeat, nothing happened.

Then came the fracture.

The chamber pulsed once then twisted. Weiss's body blurred, not disappearing, but distorting, as if seen through water. His eyes flickered. His outline fractured. He screamed once, not in pain, but in recognition of something familiar rushing in.

And then, he was gone.

∞

Chapter Six:
The Glass Between Us

∞

Darkness.

A faint hissing.
The slow hum of machinery.
Coldness biting into skin like invisible thorns.

Caelum groaned as he stirred. His eyelids were heavily drenched in sleep, memory, and something else. His hands moved first, brushing against hard surfaces.

Glass.

He blinked. Once. Twice.

The world came into focus distorted by the curve of a transparent glass chamber.

Pale blue light filtered from the ceiling above, flickering like a pulse. Thick glass surrounded him on all sides. The air smelled of rust and antiseptic. Tubes long, snaking ones ran across the ceiling like arteries, channeling soft jets of gas into his chamber. Oxygen, maybe.

He sat up slowly.

Every breath released a cloud of frost.

The room around him was cavernous and silent, but not empty.

Then he saw her.

Maaya.

In another glass chamber. A few feet away. Slumped, motionless.

For a heartbeat, panic strangled him.

"Maaya!"

His voice was muffled by the glass. But the vibration of her name seemed to reach her.

She stirred.

Lifted her head.

And when their eyes met

The chambers disappeared.

The room dissolved.

Everything faded except them.

Her face crumpled with joy and disbelief. "Caelum!"

She sprang up and stumbled to the glass, banging on it with both hands, tears spilling down her cheeks like the flood of a dam finally breaking.

Caelum pressed his palm against the glass. She mirrored it, hers trembling.

Their eyes locked not with fear, but a desperate, aching longing. A soul-deep recognition. The kind that doesn't come from days or weeks.

It felt older. Woven. Like they had found and lost each other across lifetimes.

Her lip trembled as she laughed through tears. "You're awake, you're okay. I thought I lost you."

He leaned forward, hair still damp, breath fogging the inside of his prison. "You think *you* cried? Look at me, I'm the one locked in a sci-fi fish tank."

Maaya laughed, then cried harder, then laughed again.

It echoed like fragile music in that horrific room.

A beat passed.

Then Caelum tilted his head with a smirk, a crooked, too-handsome smirk she'd memorized by now.

"Maaya" he said slowly, mock-suspicious, "Before I blacked out. I could swear I heard you calling me *darling*."

Her eyes widened in playful horror.

He pressed on with wicked delight, "Was that a hallucination or a confession?"

She sniffled, trying not to grin. "You heard nothing. You were unconscious. Delusional. Must be the oxygen tubes messing with your brain."

"Really?" he drawled, leaning against the glass. "Because it felt real."

She looked down, smiling. Then slowly, almost shyly, she looked up again, her chiffon dupatta still draped around her shoulders like a half-forgotten memory. She wiped her tears gently.

"Hum aapke hain kaun?" (who am I to you) she said, her voice low. Soft. Teasing.

Caelum blinked. "Wait, what did you just say?"

Maaya turned away theatrically. "Nothing. You imagined it. Don't ask me weird questions. Bang on the head and you're clearly daydreaming."

They both broke into laughter real, free, unguarded.

For a second, even the eerie silence of the room seemed to laugh with them.

But beneath that laughter.

Something else stirred.

The air around them buzzed faintly. A shift in pressure.
A low, clicking sound from behind the walls.
Like gears turning.
Like waking up.

Neither of them noticed. Not yet.

They were still laughing, still reaching for each other through the glass two souls tethered by something neither could name.

But as the laughter faded, a shiver ran down Maaya's spine.

Caelum noticed.

"What is it?"

She shook her head slowly. "Do you feel that?"

He paused. Listened.

And then, finally, heard it.

A voice. Metallic. Disembodied.

A recording.
From a hidden speaker.
From the shadows above.

"Subject awakening confirmed. Cycle breach detected. Initiating Sequence Δ: Memory Recall Phase One."

Maaya's hand dropped from the glass.

Caelum's heart turned cold.

Suddenly, the lights dimmed.

Their chambers hissed.

And without touching, both of them felt it:

This wasn't an accident. This was the beginning of everything.

The lights in the room flickered, humming with a strange voltage too warm, too alive. Maaya and Caelum stood inside their respective glass chambers, still catching their breath from the moment they had just shared, their fingers pressed longingly against the cold barrier between them.

And then,

The door creaked open.

Four figures entered.

Their silhouettes were long and ghostlike beneath the pale ceiling glow. Each step echoed like a countdown. Footsteps that didn't rush, didn't stumble, footsteps of those who already knew the outcome.

Maaya's heart froze.

One of the men was pushing a wheelchair.

The figure in the chair was frail, head bowed, silver hair tangled, arms resting lifelessly on the armrests. The fabric of his shirt hung loosely around bones that time had sharpened. But even in that weakened shell, she knew him.

She gasped.

A tremor ran through her body.

Then, **in Marathi**, her voice cracked like porcelain:

"Bābā? Tumhī jivanta āhāta?"
("Dad? You're… you're alive?")

She took a step forward, palm smacking against the glass. Her breath fogged instantly. "**Baba…! Baba...!**" Her voice rose with sobs. "Look at me please look at me!"

The man in the wheelchair barely stirred. His head lolled slightly to the side. His eyes were open, but distant like they were still trapped in a different year, a different world.

Then,

A mocking voice sliced through her cries like a knife through silk.

"Whatever language that was, girl, I believe I can answer it."

Yes, your father is alive.
The voice was sharp. Amused. Cruel.

Maaya turned. Maaya broke down, her fists pounding on the glass. "**Baba! Mala bagha na… mī Maaya āhe!**" (Look at me… I'm Maaya!)

Then, in a flash of rage, the Man roared

"You guinea pig, stop screaming! You're hurting my ears!"

Maaya flinched. Tears turned to fury.

Standing too still. Smiling too wide.

Her tears froze mid-air.

Before she could respond, Caelum snapped.

His voice thundered, full and unwavering.

"Don't. You. DARE. Raise your voice at her."

Caelum narrowed his eyes, a silent storm stirring behind them. "Who are you**?**" he growled, voice edged with disbelief. "Why is *her* father here? What the hell is going on?"

His eyes blazed through the glass, veins visible at his temples. "Answer me instead! How are you even alive? You were dead. You"

"You were dead, Dad!" he shouted, his voice breaking at the word.

The man turned slowly to face him.

The man smiled.

And then he laughed.

A low, guttural, vile laugh like metal dragging across bone.

It shook the floor.

Then the man leaned in, the fluorescent light catching the gleam in his eye.

"Foolish Caelum… my sweet idiot boy," he purred. "So much like your father."

"I am Azel... Azel Virek, and I'm your uncle. Not your Father."

Caelum's blood turned to ice. Caelum looked like he'd been punched in the chest.

The man took a dramatic step forward, his shadow stretching across the floor like a monster escaping its cage.

"Identical twin," he said, grinning like the devil himself. "Born seven seconds after your dad. Not that it mattered. Seven seconds was all I needed to be better. Smarter. Cursed with his face but none of his weakness."

He laughed again louder, unhinged, a laugh that climbed into the vents and shook the glass around them.

Caelum's fists slammed against the glass so hard his knuckles bled.
"How come I never knew that my father had an identical twin! You're lying!"

But he wasn't.

At that moment both Maaya and Caelum knew.

This wasn't a stranger playing a game.

This was something deeper.
Sicker.
Older.

A man with their blood.

And a secret big enough to bend time itself.

The uncle's eyes flicked from one glass prison to another.

Azel's footsteps echoed like a metronome of dread as he paced before the glass chambers, his silhouette split in half by the pale blue lights that pulsed overhead. Maaya stood frozen in disbelief, her eyes flickering between her unresponsive father and Caelum. Caelum, on the other hand, was seething fists clenched, breath fogging the glass.

Then… came the voice again.

Slick, venom-laced, theatrical.

"So… my two little guinea pigs."
Azel grinned, the word twisting off his tongue with gleeful cruelty.

He spread his arms, as if preparing to step onto a stage. His reflection danced in the chamber walls too many faces, too many shadows.

"Let me… tell you a story."
His tone shifted low and slow, the kind that coils around your spine.

"Not just any story, mind you. This one's better than all those overpriced sci-fi blockbusters you waste your weekends on."

He leaned closer to the chamber glass, his eyes gleaming like wet coal.

"A tale of *drama, thrill, suspense, love, betrayal…* and hmmm... of course death well...well murder to be precise.
He gave a smirk that suggested otherwise.

Maaya's breath hitched. Caelum's jaw tightened.

Azel stood tall now, gaze flickering between them like a pendulum of fate. His voice lowered to a growl.

"Sounds like the perfect bang-on story, doesn't it?"

Then he took one step forward.

"But..."
A pause. A dangerous, deliberate pause.

"You'd be fools to think it's a story at all."

His eyes darkened. The voice turned razor-sharp.

"Because what I'm about to tell you... is not fiction. It is the darkest, most extreme reality of your past... and the storm that's about to destroy your future."

He tilted his head and whispered:

"Lights."

And suddenly

The room began to change.

Azel started with a softer voice,

I remember the night I was born, though not through memory of my own. The story was stitched into me by whispers, by silences that carried more truth than words.

It was a night of cold rain and wind that shook the shutters like angry fists. Somewhere in the great stone house of Leonhardt Virek, two cries were meant to echo... but one never came.

Catherine, my mother no, the woman I believed to be my mother was in her own chamber miles away, giving birth under a roof that leaked and walls that trembled with every howl of the storm. She delivered stillness, a child who would never open her eyes.

And in that same hour, Leonhardt's wife brought forth life. Two lives. Twins. Seven seconds apart. Elias first and then me.

I have been told Leonhardt stood in the doorway of Catherine's chamber that night, soaked to the bone, his eyes red not from the rain. She sat there, broken, cradling emptiness in her arms. He did not speak for a long while. When he finally did, his voice was raw.

Catherine… take him. Take the younger one.

Her gaze lifted, uncomprehending. What are you saying?

He is yours now. You will tell no one. Not even my wife.

I do not know what Catherine saw in his face to make her accept. Perhaps it was the same thing I have carried my whole life: guilt mixed with love, a poison that does not kill but corrodes slowly.

And so, I was given away. Not abandoned to strangers, but worse to blood that would never feel the same. Leonhardt's wife, my true mother, lived her life believing she bore only one son: Elias. She never looked for me because she never knew I existed.

Catherine's husband, the man I was made to call father, was a drunkard. His love was measured in bottles, his kindness in rare, accidental glances. He never struck me without reason, but reasons were plentiful in that house. Catherine tried to shield me. She would whisper in the dark, Azel, you are mine. You will always be mine. I wanted to believe her, but the words rang hollow when he stumbled in the smell of cheap spirits.

It was on a winter afternoon that the truth spilled from his mouth, bitter and sharp. He had been drinking since morning. His eyes were small, mean, and fixed on me like I was something rotting in his house.

You think you're mine, boy? You're not even my blood. Your real father's name is Virek. Leonhardt Virek. He gave you away like a dog nobody wanted.

I remember my voice cracking. You're lying.

He laughed, a sound that hurt my ears. Ask your mother.

Catherine's silence that night was worse than any confession. She would not meet my eyes. That was the moment my life split into before and after.

I found them soon after Leonhardt and Elias. I did not go to them. I watched from the shadows, from the corners of streets, from the edges of gardens. Elias in fine clothes, riding horses I could only dream of. Leonhardt with the posture of a man who had never once feared where his next meal would come from.

And me… wearing the same coat for three winters.

Every day, I weighed the life I had against the life that should have been mine. Every smile they shared, every coin they spent without thought, was a theft of what I had been denied. The anger began as a thread, and over years, it became a rope around my throat.

I made myself a promise the night I saw Elias laughing by the firelight while I shivered behind the hedge.

A promise spoken only to the dark.

One day, you will both know what it feels like to be stripped of everything.

That night, the wind carried my words away. But I know it heard me.

Azel's voice fell to a hush, the kind of quiet that makes the air feel heavier. His gaze lingered on Caelum, and for a moment it was as if he were peeling back not just the years but the very walls around them.

"Do you understand now?" he said, almost tenderly. "This is not some story spun to pass the time. Every word I have given you is a shard of glass from a mirror that was broken long before you were born. You think it is the past. But it will reach into your future like a shadow that never lifts."

Caelum opened his mouth, but nothing came out. His throat was dry.

Azel leaned closer, his voice low enough to make Caelum lean in without meaning to.

"And now…" He straightened, almost smiling. "Now, let us speak of another chapter. One about a demon who thought he could wear the mask of an angel. Who tried, oh yes… but failed. Failed so miserably that it would be almost pitiful if it weren't so laughable."

His lips curled, and suddenly he let out a bark of laughter that echoed through the room, wild and unrestrained.

"Such a stupid, pea-headed brain," he said between bursts of laughter. "Ah, Leon Weiss…!" He drew out the name like a knife sliding from its sheath. "Always so certain the world would kneel for his good intentions. Always so blind to the truth that no one escapes the dirt clinging to their own hands."

For a moment, the laughter died, and his eyes hardened. "You will see him soon enough, Caelum. And when you do, you will understand that my story was not about me at all… It was about everyone who thought they could choose their own fate."

Azel's eyes narrowed as if he were seeing not Caelum but the memory of a thousand nights before. His voice lowered, not from weariness, but from the weight of what he was about to unveil.

"With anger and revenge burning inside me, I kept my distance… but never my gaze. I learned the way my real father walked, the way his voice curved when he spoke, the exact way he placed his hand on the shoulder of strangers as if the world belonged to him. I was waiting for the day his perfect little kingdom would crack. I told myself that when it did, I would be the hammer that split it open."

He leaned back, shadows sliding across his face.

"But then…" Azel's lips thinned. "I began to notice… things. Quiet meetings in dim corridors. Letters without names. Strange men arriving at night, leaving before dawn. And always… always that same insignia." His voice dropped to a whisper. "Ordo Aevi Éternum."

Caelum frowned, the name lingering in the air like incense.

"At first," Azel continued, "I thought it was nothing but another circle of greedy men gorging themselves on secrets.

But I was always sharper than your daydreamer poet father... sharper than any of them."

His fingers drummed against the table, slow, deliberate.

"I disguised myself. Took the name of no importance. A floor cleaner. That is all they saw. A man with a mop and a limp, telling the guard at the door a poor, pathetic story."

A faint smile touched his mouth, bitter as burnt wine. I told the guard, 'Sir,' one stormy night, 'I lost my home. My mother is gone and my father died in an accident. I'll clean your floors for half the wage, only... don't turn me away.' The guard had looked at me, then sighed. 'Fine. Keep your head down. Speak to no one.'

'Of course,' I'd said. 'No one at all.'

He let out a short, sharp laugh. "And while they ignored me, I saw everything."

Azel's gaze shifted to some distant, invisible point. "That is when I first saw him. Leon Weiss. A man with eyes like cold steel, and a smile that said he had already buried you in his mind. I thought, here he is. My weapon. This one is as selfish, as venomous as I am. And yes... he was. His face betrayed an ill intention the moment I studied it. I decided then he would be my knife aimed at Leonhardt Virek."

The faintest flicker of excitement passed through Azel's voice before it hardened again.

"But as I kept listening from behind half-open doors, reading scraps they thought were discarded, I began to understand... This was more than a feud, more than family revenge. They were working on something… something far ahead of its time. Something to do with time itself. And it would change the world. Not just change it… but break it, if they wished."

He paused, and his eyes locked on Caelum's.

"That was the moment I realized… my revenge was no longer enough. If I played this right, I could hold the threads of everything they were weaving and decide whether the world itself would burn."

A figure who lingered too often near my father. Leon Weiss, I was noticing. At first, he was only a shadow at the edge of my sight, but then those eyes betrayed him. Restless, hungry, timid yet sharp, the eyes of a fox waiting for the right moment to pounce. My father seemed tied to him through the same work, perhaps even trust, yet there was something in Leon Weiss that breathed beyond loyalty. He was not just a colleague. He carried in his gaze a secret purpose, something he hid from all, something that did not belong to my father or the Order but only to himself.

Azel's lips curved into that unnerving smile again, the kind that made silence tremble in the room. His finger, long and deliberate, pointed straight at Maaya.

"Hey, young lady… my beautiful little guinea pig," he drawled, his voice a mix of mockery and twisted affection. "Listen carefully, for what I am about to tell you will claw at your soul. I will now uncover the scariest, the most monstrous truth of your life. A tale of a man who wore treachery like second skin yet dared to paint himself as a saint. Brace yourself."

He threw his head back and laughed, the sound echoing like glass shattering in the dark. Then, leaning forward, his eyes gleamed with wicked delight.

“And this… is the story of Leon Weiss.”

Maaya’s breath caught in her throat, her hands instinctively clutching the edge of her chair as if to anchor herself, her wide eyes flickering with dread and disbelief at the name that suddenly felt like a curse carved into the air.

Darkness. That was Leon Weiss's first memory. Not the comforting kind of night, but a cavernous, echoing silence where time felt absent.

Leon lost his parents when he was barely five. A tragic avalanche buried them in the Swiss Alps, leaving him a trembling orphan clinging to frostbitten memories. He was raised briefly in an orphanage tucked away in the hills of Lucerne, where snow whispered at the windows and loneliness howled in the halls.

But fate hadn’t abandoned him completely. An aunt, Elisabeth Weiss, a childless widow with trembling hands and a warm heart, adopted him. She loved him like her own flesh and blood. Tucked away in a modest home near Lake Geneva, they lived quietly, tenderly. She would hum old Swiss lullabies, brush his hair with lavender oil, and whisper, "You are not broken, Leon. You are just... waiting to bloom."

But the cruelty of life is rarely spent in one strike.

Elisabeth died of liver cirrhosis when Leon was just sixteen. One evening she coughed, the next she bled. And within weeks, he was alone again the scent of lavender replaced by sterile hospital sheets and funeral lilies.

But pain shaped him. Not into anger, but into focus.

Leon worked tirelessly, fueled by grief and genius. He studied temporal physics, advanced mathematics, and quantum cosmology. Scholarships followed like shadows. He earned his doctorate in record time and was soon recruited by a secretive scientific order that operated in whispers: Ordo Aevi Éternum.

There he met Dr. Leonhardt Virek, another brilliant but tormented soul. Together they formed a brotherhood of thought, digging into ancient texts, codes, forgotten monastic archives searching for something humanity had always chased but never tamed:

Time.

Their turning point came on an expedition to Tibet, in search of the final scroll, an artifact rumored to contain the resonance laws of the Kalachakra. At the monastery's highest chamber, they found the scroll but its guardian, a wizened monk, saw through Leon's hunger.

He denied access.

And in that moment, Leon Weiss, orphaned twice by the world, made a decision that would fracture time itself.

He killed the monk.

That act would cost him everything.

With the scroll in hand, Weiss and Virek returned to Switzerland and deciphered its secrets. If two calendar years mirrored each other—1941 and 2025—during rare planetary alignments, time could be bent.

But more than math was required. Time needed a push, an emotional catalyst.

The answer? Love. Memory. Blood ties.

They called it: Resonance Convergence.

To test it, they needed a bloodline sample. Weiss volunteered. On the Omega Solstice of 1941, the loop was activated.

But the system cracked.

Weiss was flung into a liminal rift, a time limbo. Outside of clocks, outside of aging. His body reversed. His memory fragmented. He reemerged decades later in the early 1990s, not a man, but a youth.

Disoriented. Hungry. Lost.

In Delhi.

He scribbled advanced equations on broken walls using brick shards. That's where Dr. Vishwajit Deshmukh found him baffled, awed. He offered food. Shelter. But all Weiss could mutter was a mantra:

"**Yadi kāla nāsti**..."

(If time does not exist.)

A week later, Deshmukh was ambushed by local goons in a rainy alley. Weiss leapt into the fray, defending him. He fought fiercely, almost savagely and took a brutal blow to his left arm. Wounded, fevered, Weiss collapsed.

Deshmukh took him home. Bandaged him. Fed him. That night, Weiss burned in fever and murmured equations in his sleep. Sanskrit verses. Astronomical dates.

And when Deshmukh's wife, **Reena,** returned after months of healing from a tragic accident, she saw the boy and broke down screaming:

"**Mājhyā bāḷā! Tū parata ālāsa!**"

(My child! You have come back!)

Two years ago, their only son, **Aniruddh**, died in a horrific car crash. Since then, Meena had deluded herself into believing he was alive in a boarding school.

Seeing Weiss was like destiny's cruel trick.

Deshmukh, torn between truth and love, let her believe. He owed that boy his life. And perhaps, the boy needed this life too.

And from then on, "**Leon Weiss became Aniruddh Deshmukh**."

Azel's laughter split the silence, raw and jagged, echoing through the walls like a cruel hymn. His eyes burned with venomous delight as he leaned closer, each word meant to pierce her soul.

"Maaya… Leon Weiss is no stranger, no phantom carved by fate. **He is your father**. Your Aniruddh Deshmukh. The man you worshipped in memory, the man your mother wrapped in soft prayers he wore another face, another name. Leon Weiss."

The words struck like thunder.

Maaya's chest clenched. The name felt like a dagger, tearing apart the fragile threads of every story she had ever believed. Her knees trembled as if the earth itself recoiled from the truth.

"No…" the whisper escaped her lips, trembling, broken. "No, you're lying…"

Azel only laughed louder, tilting his head back, the sound cruel and endless. "Lying? Oh, my sweet guinea pig, I haven't even started. This is only the first crack in the glass. Wait until the rest shatters."

He grew up in Pune, loved dearly by both Reena and Vishwajit. He was sent to the best school, read voraciously, but remained... quiet. Withdrawn. Haunted by something even he didn't fully understand.

Years later, he became a theoretical physicist at the **University of Calcutta**, met the enchanting Meera, and married her. They had a daughter, Maaya. His life felt whole.

Until the memories returned.

Firstly, in sleep. Then, while awake. Then numbers, dates, planets, names flashing before his eyes.

One day he collapsed on the university stairs. Fell into a week-long coma.

And within that abyss of stillness, he saw it all.

The loop. The murder. The scroll. Virek. The limbo. His rebirth.

When he woke, he ran.

He returned to Pune. Tried to act normal. To be a father. Husband. Son. But he knew too much.

He was no longer just Leon. Or Aniruddh. He was both.

And he had broken time.

His heart tore between two worlds. His adopted father. His loving wife. His daughter's tiny hand gripped his finger.

He couldn't look them in the eye without breaking.

That evening, he stood by Meera as she folded laundry, Maaya sleeping on the sofa.

"You're quiet these days," she said, not looking at him.

He smiled faintly.

"Just... trying to hold on to every moment."

"That sounds ominous."

"That sounds like me."

She laughed. "You're terrible at being dramatic."

He leaned in, kissed her temple, whispered: "I love you more than time itself."

Later that night, he slipped a letter under Meera's pillow addressing both Maaya and Meera:

To my star and my axis... "Never doubt you are loved. Even when I'm not there, I am everywhere. I am going for a research expedition, see you all soon.And give my regards to Baba also."

He watched them sleep one last time. Meera's soft breathing. Vishwajit's arm hanging off the bed. Meera curled around Maaya like a shield of light.

Leon aka Aniruddh stepped out.

And vanished into the past.

To finish what he started.

To close the loop.

After hearing all these, Maaya felt the ground tilt beneath her feet. Her lungs fought for air, yet each breath only carried more dread inside her chest. She wanted to speak, to protest, to demand but her voice betrayed her, caught between fear and disbelief.

Azel leaned closer, whispering as though confessing to the earth itself.

“Leon Weiss… ah, I found him long before he became your father and trusted him. He wore hunger in his eyes. He pretended to serve others, yet his pulse throbbed with secret purpose. I knew then, he was a thread I could pull.”

His grin sharpened.

“But Maaya… you think your father disappeared by accident? That foolish little diary in Pune, the one soaked with half-truths and shadows, making your family believe Aniruddh was swallowed by fate? That was me. My gift. I made sure the world believed he had vanished into thin air.”

“And while they mourned their phantom, I rebuilt what he tried and failed,” Azel’s voice deepened, carrying both venom and triumph. One by one I murdered all the fellow scientists who were working with my Dad and your father. I didn't want to leave any trail behind, who could come and claim my throne which I have planned to build.

"You think I built this machine to heal time? To mend what was broken?" His lips curved into a cruel smile.

"No. I want no torn tapestry stitched back together. I want to rip it apart, thread by thread, and weave it anew. Mine. A history written in my hand, a future bent to my design. I was never loved by anyone nor I fell for anybody. Love made your father stupid but I am not as foolish as your father."

He stepped closer, eyes fever-bright, voice dripping with fanatic hunger.

"With the success of this experiment, I will not simply visit the past or glimpse the future. I will **own them**. I will bend centuries like branches. Rewrite kings and wars. Unmake heroes and crown villains. And whenever I desire, I will turn back the clock and do it all again."

His grin sharpened, flashing like the blade of a knife.

"I will be the first sovereign of time itself. Nations will fall at my feet not by armies, but by my command of their very beginnings. The dead will never have lived, the unborn will march in chains, and history will kneel to me."

The words clung to the air like poison, the chamber thick with his madness. Maaya's stomach twisted, bile rising as if her body itself rejected his vision. Caelum's fists clenched, bloodied, his whole frame trembling with the urge to strike but the glass, and Azel's men, held him back.

Azel laughed, a jagged sound that filled the hollow space.

"I am not a healer of time. I am its tyrant. Its executioner. And when the world learns what I have done, they will understand there was never fate. Only me."

Azel's hand hovered over the machine's core, its metallic veins pulsing faintly like something half-alive, half-starved. His voice dropped into a reverent hiss.

"But it needs more than mechanics. More than gears and equations."

His eyes shifted toward Maaya, then Caelum, glimmering with a predator's delight. "It needs blood. His blood and Yours too."

He jabbed a finger at Maaya.

And with Caelum's cursed gift braided into it, the circle will not just close it will ignite. A door not to mend what was broken, but to unmake and remake all that ever was."

Caelum strained against the guard's grip; his breath ragged with fury.

"You're insane! You can't just carve history like clay. Do you even hear yourself? You'll destroy everything!"

Azel tilted his head, mock sympathy etched on his face.

"Destroy? No, boy. I will *be liberated*. Why should I suffer the scraps of life when I can devour the whole feast? Why should kings, prophets, and fools write the story when I can hold the quill?"

"You're playing **God**!" Caelum spat, blood still trickling from his split lip. "You'll tear the world apart for your ego."

Azel's laugh was sharp, hollow, echoing like shattering glass.

"God? No. Gods wait for worship. I demand obedience. And as for the world, tell me, Caelum was it ever kind to me? Was it kind to you? To her?" His finger curled toward Maaya, whose face was pale, her breath trembling.

Caelum's eyes burned, his voice low, trembling not with fear but with raw defiance.

"If you touch her… if you use her… I swear I'll kill you, even if it breaks me."

Azel leaned in, his whisper colder than stone.

"Ah, the fire of youth. But fire without fuel dies. Remember this Caelum; blood, love, power they are the only currencies time accepts. And soon, you will give me all three."

He tilted his head, his smile widening as if he fed on their fear.

"But you must know, Maaya, your father… ah, your father was supposed to be my ally. I saw hunger in his eyes once, the same gnawing hunger that kept me alive through the filth of my youth. I thought he would help me exact my revenge. But… he failed me. Just like all the rest."

Azel's laughter cracked through the silence, hollow, merciless. He pressed his palm against the glass wall separating him from Caelum and Maaya, as if their closeness was a taunt.

"My father, Leonhardt Virek" his voice twisted around the name like a knife was a monument of honesty, cloaked in righteousness, yet he betrayed me the moment he gave me away.

A pause. His grin sharpened, his voice dipped into venom.

"Ah, destiny was always cruel to me. I thought I will never be able to claim what I was denied. I will not be able to achieve what I deserve. And then I began by cleansing the world of those who had wronged me."

"I killed my father and my brother. With the same poison, sweet and silent, so that the world would believe their hearts simply betrayed them. Natural deaths, they thought. But it was my hand, my justice."

The words detonated inside Caelum.

He surged forward, his fists clenched, his whole-body trembling with rage.

"You" his voice cracked with fury, "you killed my father… and my grandfather?" He lunged, ready to strike, but Azel's bodyguard intercepted him, slamming a fist into Caelum's gut.

Caelum staggered but didn't break, blood dripping from his lip as he spat, voice searing with hatred.

"You bastard! I'll kill you with my own hands!"

Azel's laughter split the air again, shrill and triumphant.

"Calm yourself, boy. They had to die. It was their penance for what they did to me. They deserved nothing less."

Caelum roared back, his voice tearing with grief and rage.

"Maybe my grandfather was guilty, maybe he cursed you by giving you away. But what had my father done? Why him? Why did you take him from me?"

Azel's eyes darkened, his grin vanishing into something colder, deadlier.

"He had every happiness that was meant to be mine. Wealth. Power. Family. The laughter of a mother's voice. The legacy of a father's name. And don't you know, boy?"

His voice grew into a thunderous snarl.

"The child must bear the sins of their parents. Haven't you heard that before?"

His hand struck the glass with sudden violence, the chamber vibrating with the force.

"Do not interrupt me again!" he roared, the sound filling the room like a curse.

Silence felt heavy, broken only by Caelum's ragged breathing and Maaya's muffled sob. Azel leaned back, his smile returning, curling with wicked delight.

His eyes gleamed, fever-bright.

"Though my father had tried, oh how he tried, to undo the experiment, to claw back what was lost, to bring back his friend Leon. Every day he failed, and every failure drove him deeper into madness. He crumbled, rotting from sorrow, until death took him. But Leon Weiss... I don't know where he went. Dead or alive. But I still had the belief that he still lived. He was the thread of fate I needed."

Azel's tone turned mocking, cruelly playful.

"Then I planned to take advantage of my father's mental condition and I approached him gently, oh so sweetly, with a son's voice. I told him how I missed him. How I suffered. I made him believe we shared the same wounds. And the fool believed me. He even confessed he said he searched for me but could not find me."

Azel's laughter spilled out again, sharp and merciless.

"Who would believe such a lie? If he had truly wanted to, he would have found me. No, he only wanted to salve his guilt."

He leaned forward, eyes narrowing with wicked pride.

"From him I took everything. His notes. His secrets. His blood, too. And when he was of no further use, I poured him a cup of poisoned coffee. Sweet, silent, painless. Or perhaps not so painless… I enjoyed watching the disbelief in his eyes. The betrayal. The anguish. It tasted sweeter than any wine."

Caelum, battered but unbroken, shouted through the glass, voice hoarse with fury.

"You bastard!"

The bodyguard struck him again, knuckles cracking against his face, and blood spilled from Caelum's nose. He spat it onto the floor, glaring with fire.

Unmoved, Azel continued, his voice almost reverent.

Though I had almost everything to rebuild what they couldn't achieve with their minds. With my father's wealth, I grew powerful. I bought this place, stone by stone. And I built what they could not. I made the machine better with my sharp intellegence, the only thing that I have inherited naturally from my family. The machine that will tear time apart and sew it back as I wish. I crowned myself king of eternity."

"I tried using different subjects but failed as I knew I was missing out on something really very important. And then one day when I was thinking of giving up , fate threw me a **gift**. On the streets of Switzerland, in the cold gutters, begging like a dog I found your father, Leon Weiss."

"Ah, the man the world thought was dead. I thought so too with the passing years, until I saw him. Shattered. Sick. A ghost of what he once was. I gave him aid to get a little better and earned his trust to help him close the loop.

His voice broke into bitter laughter.

"I thought now with Leon's help I will finally achieve what I want. But the machine was cruel. It demanded sacrifice. Love. Blood. Things I did not have, things I had lost long ago. So, I failed. Again."

"A man who has already been part of the experiment cannot be chosen twice. Leon's turn was spent, his role exhausted. He was nothing but a broken remnant."

"Your foolish father saw through my plans and dared to defy me. So I withdrew the lifeline he depended on and now, Maaya, behold what's left of him… a hollow shell, a withered remnant of the man he once was."

His eyes flashed with something darker, something fevered.

Azel spread his arms wide, his grin splitting his face.

"And then—then the idea came. The most beautiful idea. You two. Caelum and Maaya. The children of two lines entangled with eternity. The perfect sacrifice. The perfect key. With your blood, your bond, your power I will finish what has begun. I will make the world mine. And I will laugh as time itself kneels."

The chamber seemed to grow colder, the shadows tightening around them. Maaya pressed trembling palms against the glass, her breath catching, her tears spilling unchecked. Caelum staggered to his feet, his fury undimmed, his body shaking with the weight of rage and disbelief.

And Azel laughed. A sound that no longer belonged to any man, echoing like a curse against the bones of the earth.

∞

Chapter Seven: The Hour When Time Screamed

∞

The chamber smelled of copper, smoke, and fear. Azel stood over the machine a monstrous weave of wires, spinning gyros, and clocks that ticked against each other, faster than a heartbeat. At its center, the Seal glowed, pulsing with an unnatural light, as if time itself had been forced into a cage.

Maaya was bound to the chair, her violet eyes burning with terror, her breath ragged. The straps cut into her wrists, crimson threads blooming across her skin. The machine hummed louder, and the room trembled.

Caelum staggered forward, his silver eyes wild, hair plastered to his face with sweat. His body shook not from fear, but from fury.

"You don't understand Azel," Caelum's voice was both sharp and trembling.

"Whatever you are saying if it's true then as per my understanding the loop must close. One bloodline, one sacrifice will balance the equation."

"I am ready to sacrifise but please leave Maaya. You're killing her!" Caelum roared. His voice cracked the silence like thunder.

"No, I'm recreating the world." Azel's hand twisted the dial. Sparks burst, filling the room with white fire.

Maaya screamed, the sound splitting Caelum open from the inside. He lunged, but a sudden crash of movement stopped him.

Leon Weiss aged, trembling, but fiercely stepped between them. His chest heaved, eyes locked on Azel.

"Not her," Leon said, his voice breaking but steady.

"You'll have to kill me first."

Azel's lips curled. "So be it."

The strike came quickly. A blade of pure energy arced from the machine, slicing through the air. Leon took it full in the chest. His body jolted, blood blooming scarlet across his shirt. Maaya shrieked, straining against her bonds, while Caelum dropped to his knees beside him.

"Baba..." Maaya's voice was a child's again raw, broken.

Leon's trembling hand reached for his daughter's. "Protect her... Caelum... She is your axis. Not the Seal. Not the loop. Her." His last breath rattled, then stilled.

The silence that followed was unbearable.

Something inside Caelum snapped. He looked up at Azel, and for the first time, his silver eyes blazed not with memory, but with power.

"You wanted a fracture?" Caelum growled. "Then watch me break it."

With a roar that seemed to come from centuries, he tore free of doubt. Every scar, every loss, every dream of Maaya's violet eyes wove into strength. He surged toward the machine. His fingers closed around the Seal.

Azel shouted, "Don't you dare!"

Maaya screamed, "You'll kill yourself!"

But Caelum looked at her looked through time itself and whispered,

"I would break a thousand timelines for you Maaya." And he crushes the Seal in his hand.

The explosion is blinding.

The world **convulses**. Every clock on the planet stutters, every digital screen glitches at once, satellites flicker out of orbit. The streets of 2025 erupt in chaos, sirens wail, car alarms shriek, and skyscraper windows shatter as shock waves ripple through the city.

Maaya feels her body pulled apart, stretched across a thousand possibilities, as if her very soul is being rewritten in real time. People outside must have felt this exertion too.

Through it all, Caelum's arms wrap around her, shielding her from the storm.

"I will love you in every year," he breathes against her hair, before pressing his mouth to hers. The kiss is bruising, desperate, a tether in the chaos.

Azel's scream cuts through the maelstrom. His body is sucked into the collapsing loop, dragged toward the machine that spins like a black hole. His face twists in fury as his form dissolves into fragments of light and data, scattering into the collapsing fabric of 2025.

"You think you've won?" Azel howled.

"This is not the end! Even if I vanish, the story is not complete. I will return. And when I do, I will tell you the real story, the one I haven't told to my any dearest!"

His laughter echoed as he vanished, swallowed whole by the devouring loop.

Then silence.
Time folded shut.

The chamber screamed as if the earth itself were breaking apart. Stone and fire rained from the ceiling, dust clawed into Maaya's lungs, and the glowing shards of the Seal flickered like dying constellations around them.

Caelum's body was her shield. His arms, bruised and trembling, caged her from the avalanche of rock. She could feel the tremor of his muscles, the warmth of his chest pressed to hers, even as blood spilled from the gash across his temple. His silver eyes, once blazing with strength, fluttered half-closed.

For one terrible heartbeat, Maaya felt the world go silent.

No breath. No pulse. Nothing.

Her soul tore open.

"Caelum!" Her scream ripped through the ruins. She shook him, her violet eyes drowning in tears, her voice hoarse with terror. "Don't you dare leave me! Don't you dare!"

His lashes quivered. A flicker of silver. His lips parted.

"Run…" The word was barely air, a ghost of command.

"I won't!" Maaya sobbed, clutching his face with shaking hands. "Do you hear me? I will not leave you. I would rather die here with you than breathe a single second without you."

But the chamber groaned like a monster awakening. Cracks tore through the floor, swallowing shadows whole. The roar of collapsing stone grew deafening.

Adrenaline surged. Maaya dragged him, stumbling, her limbs screaming, her throat raw with ash and grief. Every step was a war, every breath a prayer. She pulled him into the collapsing passage, her body half-carrying, half-dragging his weight.

And then came the thunderclap of doom.

The roof above buckled with a roar, a slab of stone splitting from the heavens. Caelum, with the last of his strength, thrust her forward. His hands pushed her into the night, into the thin sliver of freedom beyond the collapsing arch.

Her scream split the air.

"Caelum! No"

She fell into the cold night wind, coughing, blinded by tears. The earth heaved beneath her, the chamber exploding in dust and rubble behind. She scrambled to her feet, choking, clawing through the haze. But when she turned back there was nothing.

Only silence. Only ruins. Only darkness where he had been. Maaya's knees buckled. Her scream tore through the mountains, raw and unearthly, her voice breaking into sobs that shook her chest.

"CAELUM!"

Her violet eyes searched the smoke for even a flicker of silver. But the night had swallowed him whole.

Maaya had been grieving every breath, every heartbeat since the collapse. Each night she lay awake, clawing at memories of silver eyes that had burned for her in the chamber before the dust swallowed him whole. Every second in Switzerland was a wound, every corner of the city whispered his absence.

The world felt uninhabitable without him. His laughter haunted her; his touch lingered on her skin like fire. And when she could bear it no more, when the weight of Switzerland became unbearable, she booked her flight.

The airport was a blur, voices echoing like ghosts, glass walls reflecting her loneliness back at her. Her hands trembled as she clutched her boarding pass. Her violet eyes, rimmed red with sleepless grief, stared at nothing. She moved like a woman half-dead, a sleepwalker abandoning the ruins of her heart.

And then—

"Akele hi chali jaaogi, Señorita?"

The words boomed through the air in clumsy Hindi, but achingly familiar. It pierced her like lightning. She froze. Her chest seized. Slowly, almost fearfully, she turned.

Her world stopped.

There he was. Standing not far away, bruised, blood still dried at his temple, shirt torn, arm wrapped in bandages. But alive. *Alive.* His silver eyes found her in the crowd, steady, burning, as if they had been searching only for her.

"Caelum..." Her voice cracked apart, half-sob, half-prayer.

The boarding pass slipped from her fingers. Her bag crashed to the floor. None of it mattered. She ran wild, unstoppable, heart beating louder than the announcements above.

He caught her mid-flight. His arms crushed her against him, strong despite his wounds. And then their lips met. No hesitation. No words. A desperate, consuming kiss, so hard, so hungry, it tasted of salt and grief and resurrection. Her tears poured against his mouth as she clung to him, her nails digging into his back as though she could anchor him to this world by force alone.

She pulled away only to sob against his lips, whispering in broken Marathi, *"Murkhā mulgā, I thought you were gone… My world—my world was shattered."*

He kissed her again, slower this time, lips trembling against hers as if promising eternity in that moment. "No, Maaya," he breathed, his forehead pressed to hers. "I'm here. And I'm coming with you."

Her violet eyes searched his silver ones, disbelieving, desperate. "But your life here, your mother?"

He smiled faintly, bruised but radiant. "I've arranged everything. My work, my home… even my mother. She will live hers, she always did, without me. But I—I only began living the day I met you. All these years, I was a shadow. With you, I am real."

Her tears spilled harder. She buried her face against his chest, sobbing, yet laughing through the ache. "So, what will I tell my mother? Who are you to me?"

He chuckled, brushing his lips against her hair, his breath warm and tender. "That, Maaya… is for you to decide."

She lifted her face, eyes gleaming, lips trembling into a smile. "And what will you do in India?"

His silver eyes blazed, brighter than the airport lights. "The most important work of my life."

She tilted her head, teasing through her tears. "Which is?"

He cupped her face, kissed her once more, deep and slow, before murmuring against her lips—

"To love you."

Back in Pune

The stone bungalow at Bhukum was alive with whispers the moment Maaya stepped inside with Caelum. The air carried the scent of sandalwood and old grief, but that night it trembled with something else, hope and fear colliding.

Meera stood in the doorway. Her anklets, once the heartbeat of the house, lay silent at her feet. For a heartbeat she only stared at her daughter, as if afraid that the vision before her might dissolve into smoke.

Then, suddenly, Meera's palm cracked across Maaya's cheek. The sound echoed through the verandah like a shattering of silence. Maaya gasped, stunned but before she could react, Meera collapsed into tears, clutching her daughter's face, covering it in frantic kisses like she was a little girl again.

"My Maaya," Meera wept, her body shaking. "You came back. I thought… I thought I had lost you, just like your father."

Tears streamed down Maaya's own cheeks as she held her mother close. "Aai… I had to come back. How could I leave you alone? I promised you I would return. And, Aai I have so much to tell you… about Baba."

Meera cupped her daughter's face, kissed her forehead again and again. Then, with a trembling smile through her tears, she whispered, "First, freshen up, my love. Then we will talk. All night, if we must."

Only then did her gaze lift to the tall stranger standing quietly behind Maaya. Her expression shifted joy to suspicion, warmth to steel.

"Who is he, Maaya?" Her voice trembled.

Maaya's fingers instantly found Caelum's hand. She clutched it tight, her violet eyes fierce. "Aai… this is Caelum. The one who saved me. The one I… love."

The word *love* cracked the air.

Meera's tears still. Her eyes widened, clouded with fear. "Love?" she whispered hoarsely. "Your father was lost to this madness. Do you want the same fate, Maaya?"

Before Maaya could speak, Caelum stepped forward. His shirt torn, his face still carrying the bruises of their battles, he folded his hands clumsily, his voice trembling in broken Hindi but steady in feeling:

"Namaste, Aunty. Main… Maaya se bahut pyaar karta hoon. I promise… main usse akeli kabhi nahi chhodunga." (Namaste, Aunty. I love Maaya very much. I promise I will never leave her alone.)

The raw sincerity of his words, spoken with a heavy accent but burning truth, stunned Meera into silence. Her eyes darted to her daughter's trembling fingers clinging to his hand. Slowly, her fury softened into grief. She turned away, her voice a whisper of surrender:

"Bas… khush reh."

(Just… be happy.)

That night, mother and daughter sat together with Caelum, Maaya narrating everything—the saffron box, the visions, the collapse, her father's truth. Each word carved deeper lines into Meera's face. When Maaya's voice broke, Caelum took over, steady and unflinching.

By the time they finished, Meera sat like stone. Not a word. Not a tear. Her silence was heavier than screams.

Later, when Maaya tried to step into her mother's room, Caelum caught her wrist gently. "Let her vent out tonight," he murmured. "Grief is an ocean. Sometimes one must drown before they can swim again."

The next morning, Maaya woke to the sound of ankle bells. She rushed to the courtyard and stopped short.

There was Meera radiant, alive dancing again. Her ghungroos sang against the stone floor, each step a resurrection. Her face glistened with tears, but her body flowed with forgotten rhythm. Maaya's eyes filled as she joined her mother, her own steps awkward at first, then flowing. For the first time in years, the mother and daughter laughed through their tears, their hearts beating in rhythm with the music of love returned.

Later that week, Maaya dragged Caelum to the German Bakery. The bell jingled as they entered, and the aroma of coffee wrapped around them.

Aanya spotted them and nearly dropped her cappuccino. "Arre Mau!" she squealed, eyes wide. "You didn't tell me you were importing Swiss chocolate in human form!"

Caelum blinked, utterly lost. "Chocolate?"

Ravi, already sketching the moment on a napkin, chuckled. "Bollywood meets Lucerne. History just found its next scandal."

Maaya groaned. "You two, stop! He's not a showpiece."

But Caelum leaned closer to her, silver eyes mischievous, his voice low enough only for her to hear: "Maybe I am. For you."

Aanya clutched her chest dramatically. "Uff! Cheesy bhi hai! (He's cheesy too!) Maaya, he's perfect."

Ravi added with mock solemnity, "We're finished. The love triangle is complete. It's Ravi vs. Swiss Thor."

Everyone laughed, but at that moment Maaya knew her world had changed forever.

One misty evening, Professor Sudarshan arrived. His eyes lingered on Caelum for a long, heavy silence. Then he spoke, his voice low, carrying the weight of years:

"You've brought him here, Maaya. But time has a price."

Caelum bowed respectfully, his Hindi broken but firm. "Sir, I'll protect her. Always."

Sudarshan shook his head slowly. His gaze cut through both of them. "Love does not stop the clocks, Caelum. It only makes them tick louder."

The words hung in the air like an omen.

In the weeks that followed, Maaya showed Caelum her world, her Pune. At George Restaurant, he burned his tongue on sizzling hot plates, coughing furiously while Maaya laughed until her eyes watered.

"Swiss God brought down by Indian chilli," she teased. At Mastani House, she cradled her rose milkshake with reverence, sipping slowly. Caelum couldn't take his eyes off her. "How can a drink make you glow like that?" he whispered. She blushed, hiding behind the glass.

On a fog-draped morning at Sinhagad, the chill made her shiver. Without a word, he wrapped his coat around her shoulders. She leaned into him, her violet eyes soft. "This is my world, Caelum."

He pressed his lips gently to her forehead. "Now it is ours."

At Manas Lake, the violet dusk shimmered across the water. Caelum's silver eyes reflected it as he murmured, "Here, time feels alive."

Maaya smiled faintly, slipping her hand into his. "It always was. We just didn't listen."

Their Union

Theirs was a marriage built on survival, on fire and ruin, on a love that had clawed its way out of death.

Life unfolded in tender fragments after that. Caelum began teaching at Pune University. The campus had never buzzed like this before. Ever since Professor Caelum walked through those ivy-covered gates, the air seemed to shimmer differently as if even the wind stopped to listen.

Girl students were losing their minds over the new professor half in awe, half in disbelief. Every lecture hall he entered turned into a stage, every chalk stroke a performance. His voice calm, deep, and deliberate had the kind of command that made even the backbenchers sit up straight.

Riya (a random student), clutching her notebook, whispered to her friend mid-lecture, "He's not teaching... he's *casting a spell*! Look at the way he pauses between words like he's reciting poetry!"

Her friend Kritika (a random student) bit her lip, eyes still glued to the board.

"Forget poetry… if he asks a question, I'm volunteering even if I have no idea what he's talking about."

Meanwhile, the boys exchanged looks that carried the weight of silent competition. Some laughed it off, some brooded in corners pretending not to notice the stares the girls threw at Caelum.

Arjun (a random student), leaning back in his chair, muttered under his breath, "Great. Another hero professor. What's next? Fan club meetings after class?"

Dev (a random student) chuckled. "You're just jealous, bro. Admit it even you started wearing that crisp white shirt today."

But it wasn't just the students. In the staff room, even his colleagues weren't immune. The usual gossip had turned into a low hum of admiration.

Once in the faculty room, Professor Rupali, adjusting her glasses with a sigh, said, "Did you hear how he explained Nietzsche? I felt like I was listening to a TED Talk delivered by a poet."

Professor Rakesh smirked. "Careful, Meera. Next thing we know, you'll be sitting in the front row with those lovestruck students."

Caelum, however, moved through it all with effortless calm. For him, this spectacle was déjà vu. He'd seen the same flutter of fascination, the same mix of envy and admiration, back in his previous university. The world, it seemed, never tired of turning his classrooms into theatres.

And as he closed his lecture notes that day, a faint smile crossed his lips, the kind that carried both amusement and a secret he wasn't ready to tell.

Maaya, meanwhile, turned her griefs and miracles into words. Her first novel poured out of her in fevered nights and candlelit dawns a tapestry woven with time, love, and loss. Critics would one day call it haunting. But to her, it was nothing less than a confession carved in ink. She got completely consumed in it. And slowly she started behaving oddly.

It began with a knock at the door soft, hesitant, but enough to ripple through the fragile calm of the evening.

Maaya opened it to find a young student, drenched in rain, clutching a notebook. "I'm so sorry, ma'am," the girl stammered, "Professor Caelum asked me to submit my draft tomorrow, but… I couldn't wait for his feedback."

Caelum appeared behind Maaya, his voice calm, almost kind. "It's alright, Anvi. You can leave it with me."

The girl insisted, "Sir , I can wait for your feedback, that's why I rushed to your home."

Caelum replied with a firm voice, "I think it will be better for you to leave right now otherwise you will fall sick."

The girl stood silently for a few seconds and then took out a big size chocolate and offered it to Caelum saying,

Sir yesterday you mentioned during the class that you love Swiss chocolate. I couldn't manage to find one here, so instead got this for you. But I promise to bring you Swiss chocolate later on."

The girl smiled too long, too bright and left with a "Goodnight, Professor."

The door clicked shut. Silence. Then the storm inside Maaya began.

"Do all your students come to *our house* now?" she asked, her tone sweet with venom.

Caelum sighed, loosening his collar. "Maaya, it was just about her paper."

"Oh, her paper and what about the chocolate?" she snapped, pacing the room. "You didn't see the way she looked at you?"

He frowned. "You're imagining things."

Her laugh was bitter. "Imagining? I saw her eyes, Caelum. I've seen that look before the same one every other woman gives you."

He turned sharply. "And what look is that, Maaya?"

"The one that makes me feel invisible!" she burst out. "The one that reminds me you'll always belong to a world that's watching you, not to me."

He froze, the words sinking in like rain into soil. The tension crackled in the air between them raw, alive, almost dangerous.

The thunder rolled again, closer this time, shaking the windowpanes. Maaya stood by the table, her hands trembling, her anger dissolving into something far more dangerous longing mixed with fear.

Caelum took a slow step toward her. His voice was quieter now, almost breaking.

"Every time I walk into a room, people see a version of me they invented. But *you,* Maaya... you see the one I'm trying to hide."

She met his gaze, eyes glistening. "Then why do you keep shutting me out?"

He was inches away now. "Because when you look at me like that, I forget how to breathe."

The space between them pulsed with the sound of rain. A candle flickered on the table, throwing restless light over their faces. Maaya's heartbeat filled the silence.

"I hate how much you affect me," she whispered.
"Then don't fight it," he said, his voice barely more than air.

A flash of lightning lit the room for an instant, the world was pure white. And in that moment, all their anger, jealousy, and unspoken love collided. They stood motionless, too close, their words evaporating into the charged air.

He stepped closer.

She opened her mouth to reply, but the words tangled in her throat. The air between them shifted, charged, trembling. The distance that had felt like miles now felt like a breath.

Rain hammered the windows. A strand of her hair clung to her cheek, and without thinking, he reached out and brushed it away. The touch was meant to be a small truce, perhaps but it lingered longer than it should have.

Her breath caught.
His eyes softened.

The world outside blurred into sound: the storm, the wind, the soft hum of electricity between them.

"This isn't fair," she whispered.
"Neither is wanting someone this much," he
murmured back.

And in that suspended second anger dissolved. Words fell away.
What remained was the ache of everything unsaid.

When their lips finally met, it wasn't gentle, it was desperate, inevitable. The kind of kiss that rewrites history.

The storm outside roared louder, as if the heavens themselves leaned closer to listen.

And then, on one bitterly cold winter night, the world seemed to hold its breath. Frost clung to the edges of the windowpanes, and every gust of wind rattled the old house like a warning. Unwanted lightning split the sky in jagged brilliance, illuminating the hospital room in fleeting bursts of silver.

Maaya lay bundled against the chill, every shiver a testament to the fog outside and the storm within her. Caelum never left her side, his hands steadying hers, his voice low and urgent over the howling wind.

And then, as if the heavens themselves waited for this moment, a cry cut through the cold, the thunder, and the darkness a tiny, urgent sound, fragile yet fierce. Maaya had given birth to a daughter.

The newborn's first wails pierced the storm like an ancient promise fulfilled, a spark of life defying the night's icy fury. Wrapped in warmth and blankets, the baby seemed impossibly small, impossibly perfect, yet undeniably strong the first light in a night that had tested every limit of fear, hope, and love.

Caelum leaned close, his forehead resting against hers, their breaths mingling in the cold air.

"She's… perfect," he whispered, voice thick with awe.

Maaya, exhausted but radiant, smiled through tears. "Just like we dreamed… just like we hoped."

Outside, the fog began to soften, as if even the clouds themselves had bowed to welcome this new life. And in that cold, electric night, they realized that some promises -- the most important ones -- are kept not in words, but in hearts and breaths, and in the fragile cry of a newborn.

Meera wept as she held the child, her heart softened after years of jagged grief. At last, she turned to Sudarshan, her Suddu, her patient shadow and whispered out of surprise, "She has both of her parent's eyes."

But Sudarshan's smile was strange. His gaze lingered too long on the child, and when Meera asked why he grinned so darkly, his reply was soft, chilling:

"Time and tide wait for none, my love. Not even for us."

danced with her granddaughter. Caelum and Maaya, tired yet radiant, built their world brick by fragile brick.

For a while, life tricked them into believing that peace had finally found a home. The bungalow once wrapped in silence now echoed with the lilting laughter of their baby girl. Her giggles tangled with the soft chiming of ghungroos as Meera swayed across the veranda, her silver hair catching the sun.

"She has your eyes, Maaya," Meera said, spinning the little one gently in her arms. "And her smile is just like Caelum's. You were right, my love. This house needed her laughter."

Maaya watched them, her heart swelling with a warmth too tender to name. "Sometimes I think she's brought you back to being lively again, Aai," she whispered, and Meera laughed through misted eyes.

Later that night, as moonlight spilled across their room, Caelum traced circles on their daughter's tiny palm. "Can you believe she's ours?" he murmured.

"Every time she laughs, it feels like the world begins again," Maaya replied, resting her head on his shoulder.

Caelum smiled faintly, brushing a curl from her face. "You know what I keep dreaming of?"

She looked up, curious.

"A little boy," he said softly. "Running after her in this garden, making her cry, then making her laugh again."

Maaya's lips curved into a wistful smile. "Then let him come when he's ready," she whispered. "Our hearts will make room."

And in that small, golden moment, between the laughter and the lullabies, life felt whole again.

But time is never gentle with those who defy it. It began with whispers in the night. Soft at first barely audible murmurs curling through the dark, threading between dreams.

Maaya dreamt of collapsing domes, of clocks melting into ash, their faces weeping molten time. Each night the visions grew heavier, the silence afterward too sharp, too real.

Caelum woke gasping, his skin clammy with fear, eyes wide as fragments of 1941 bled into his waking mind, sirens splitting the air, buildings bowing to flame, shadows screaming through smoke and ruin.

They never spoke of it. Each morning, they exchanged quiet

smiles, pretending it was nothing more than exhaustion or the ghosts of bad memories.

They told themselves they had endured too many storms, too many unspoken truths. Surely, this was just their weary minds replaying what had once broken them.

But the nights began to lengthen. The air felt heavier. The clocks ticked louder, almost deliberate.

And somewhere in that stillness between their dreams, time began to tremble as if something long forgotten was trying to wake.

Then!

One night, lightning cracked across the sky, splitting the darkness into shards. Both of them woke at once, clutching each other, eyes wide with terror. The same visions seared their souls' bombs raining, earthquakes tearing the land apart, the saffron box glowing like a curse reborn.

"Caelum…" Maaya whispered, trembling, her voice cracking, "it's happening again."

He pulled her close, his silver eyes blazing with fear and love. "Whatever it is, we face it together." They both gazed at her daughter once with fearful eyes.

The storm outside roared louder, the child stirred in her cradle, and the air trembled with something unseen.

And then silence.

When dawn came, the cradle was still. The sheets on the bed were untouched. The house at Bhukum lay quiet, every corner heavy with absence.

Maaya and Caelum were gone.

Vanished without a trace.

Only the faint glimmer of saffron light lingered in the room, pulsing once before it, too, dissolved into the morning fog.

∞

Epilogue: The Photograph

Years later, in the shadowed stillness of a dusty antique shop in Tulshi Baug, Pune, a young girl with pearl-violet eyes wandered between forgotten relics. The air smelled of brass, old wood, and memory. Then she stopped frozen before an aged photograph resting in a cracked silver frame.

Two men stood beneath a towering clock. One cloaked in wartime lace, his expression grave; the other in modern black, his gaze almost alive through the decades.

She leaned in, heart thudding softly.

"That's… Suddu Dadu…" she whispered, disbelief trembling in her voice. The man in black young, certain, impossible—was him.

Her fingers turned the photograph over. The paper rasped, brittle with age. On the back, in hurried ink, a message sprawled like a secret never meant to be found:

"We never broke time. We made it our story. —A.S."

The shop clock began to chime twelve.

Each strike reverberated through the floorboards, through her heartbeat, through something far older than the walls. And in that suspended instant, the ticking ceased as if time itself leaned forward, curious, remembering what it once forgot.

∞

End notes

The calendar will match again. The loop never ends. And when it does, someone hungry enough and greedy enough will try to change it again.

Perhaps the Seal was never destroyed. Perhaps it only slept. And when the child with violet-silver eyes rises, she will walk through centuries to find those who were lost.

And you, my dear reader yes, you

your heartbeat may be part of her story.

"Because time always remembers
those who dared to love it back"........

Glossary

Ajoba: Grandfather (Marathi)

Aai: Mother (Marathi)

Ghungroo: Ankle-bells worn by Indian classical dancers (Hindi)

Seva: Selfless service (Hindi/Sanskrit)

Pallu: Loose end of a sari (Hindi/Marathi)

Vada Pav: Popular street food in Maharashtra (Spicy potato fritter in a bun)

Aga Bai: Oh dear! / Expression of surprise (Marathi)

Biryani: A fragrant rice dish cooked with spices, and often with vegetables, chicken, or mutton.

Sambar: A South Indian lentil-based stew made with tamarind, vegetables, and spices.

Aloo Tikki: Spiced potato patties, shallow fried until crisp, often served with chutneys.

Payasam: A traditional Indian sweet pudding made with milk, sugar or jaggery, and rice or vermicelli.

Mirchi Bhajji: Deep-fried fritters made by dipping whole green chilies in spiced gram flour batter.

Kanda Bhajji (Onion Bhajji/Pakora): Deep-fried onion fritters, spiced and crispy, made with gram flour batter.

About the Author

Miss Tanka Das is a lifelong learner whose journey bridges numbers, narratives, and nature. Armed with degrees in Commerce, Advanced Accountancy & Taxation, PGDM in Finance & Marketing, B.Ed in English, Geography & Commerce, ECCEd, and a *Visharad* in classical music, she now pursues a Master's in British & Indian Literature while completing her PhD in Finance and teaching the same at MIT-WPU, Pune. After years working in prominent MNCs and broking firms, she shifted to education, her true calling. A passionate cook, voracious reader, and eternal dreamer, she writes with one hand in finance, the other in folklore, believing beauty exists in everything and that love for nature anchors it all.